YUKI CHAN IN BRONTË COUNTRY

Mick Jackson is the prize-winning author of the novels *The Underground Man*, *Five Boys* and *The Widow's Tale*. He also published, with the illustrator David Roberts, two acclaimed curiosities, *Ten Sorry Tales* and *Bears of England*.

Further praise for *Yuki chan in Brontë Country*:

'Since winning the Authors' Club Best First Novel prize with *The Underground Man* (1997), Mick Jackson's work has been increasingly characterised by a perceptive humanity, laced with sly wit and presented with irresistible dynamism, and this is no exception.' *Financial Times*

'The psychic detective story soon becomes an engrossing one of a motherless young girl finding her way in the world and dealing with her grief.' *Big Issue North*

'All novelists want their imaginations to travel, but few send them off as far as Mick Jackson . . . It is brave for a middle-aged male Lancastrian to put himself into the mind of a young Japanese woman, and to bring such disparate elements as clairvoyance, cultural difference and the Brontës together in a story . . . they do make for an enjoyable adventure in Brontëland.' *Guardian*

'That a whimsical comedy can transmute into an elegiac exercise in the futility of pursuing catharsis is no small achievement. That it is both funny and plangent is another.' *Independent*

'Subtly haunting and strangely affecting . . . utterly authentic.' *Press Association*

'A quietly devastating study of loss that sneaks up on you.' *Country Life*

'A charming and utterly absorbing meditation on grieving and identity.' *The Lady*

'The book strikes out in unusual directions and you can't really anticipate where you are going to be taken, page by page. Yukiko is given to stray fancies, charming memories, affecting visualisations that defiantly linger in your mind after you've read them . . . this novel had an air of late period Brautigan about it [which] is very close to being the highest praise indeed.' *Bookmunch*

by the same author

The Underground Man
Five Boys
Ten Sorry Tales, illustrated by David Roberts
Bears of England, illustrated by David Roberts
The Widow's Tale

Yuki chan in Brontë Country

MICK JACKSON

FABER & FABER

First published in 2016
by Faber & Faber Limited
Bloomsbury House, 74–77 Great Russell Street
London WC1B 3DA
This paperback edition first published in 2017

Printed and bound in England by CPI Group (UK) Ltd, Croydon, CR0 4YY

A CIP record for this book
is available from the British Library

ISBN 978-0-571-25426-2

FSC
www.fsc.org
MIX
Paper from
responsible sources
FSC® C101712

2 4 6 8 10 9 7 5 3 1

Your only hope of getting a half-decent photo of the Post Office Tower is to shoot it from a distance. You can try standing directly below it, but the concrete base just gets in the way. There may be something in between these two perspectives, but Yukiko couldn't find it. Which is kind of odd, since she's long considered the Post Office Tower to be as much an icon of her beloved Swinging Sixties as Biba, The Beatles and Mary Quant.

Of course, the one surefire way of getting a great picture would be to rent a helicopter and hover over it, just off to one side. That way you'd get the height as well as the detail. Like those shots of Apollo 11, when it's sitting on the tarmac in the last few seconds before they put a match to a billion litres of rocket fuel to try and get that sucker off the ground.

It didn't take long for Yuki's sister, Kumiko, to set her straight regarding any hope of her actually going up the tower. Apparently, civilians haven't been allowed anywhere near it since about 1972. So not only is there no easy way of taking a photograph, but you can't get inside to admire all the fittings and fixtures, or take an elevator up to a viewing platform – if such a thing even exists.

There's a whole bunch of reasons why Yuki has such affection for the Post Office Tower, relating to its own peculiar beauty and the period in which it was conceived, but her Number One reason is the fact that it has one of the original revolving restaurants. Yuki gets giddy just thinking about it. Back in '69 it must have seemed like the height of sophistication to be sitting at a table eating your fancy Sixties food while the world eased slowly by you – and presumably at exactly the right speed. Because too fast and you'd be bringing up the food you'd just eaten, and too slow and you'd have finished your meal and be back in the elevator before you'd covered the full 360 degrees. Someone somewhere must have carried out research into the optimum speed of revolving restaurants. When Yuki opens her Museum of Interesting Things she plans to make it a priority to track down all those technical drawings and data and have them displayed in pride of place.

Anyway, the fact that the restaurant hasn't moved in several decades is, in Yukiko's opinion, pretty much an International Tragedy. Not least, since high-altitude revolving restaurants now seem to be just about everywhere. The old Post Office Tower could show some of these new kids how it's meant to be done. Yuki has put some thought into how she might sneak up there and get it going. Rather than waste time trying to crawl in through the air-con or sewage system, she's decided the trick is to just show up with a dozen or so like-minded comrades, all dressed in their Sixties skirts and frilly blouses, with their Vidal Sassoon haircuts, giggling and carrying bottles of champagne – as if they've just emerged from their own little time machine. Then just swan right past the security guy, stumble into the elevator, and – still giggling – zip on up to whatever floor the restaurant's on.

It might take a little while to locate the light switches, and a little while longer to get the thing moving again. Yuki likes to imagine there's just some great big lever. Then that old turntable will slowly grind back into action, and she and her pals will take their snacks out of their handbags and have a little picnic, gazing out over the city, pretending that it's 1969 down there.

In fact, having encountered the tower up close, Yuki now sees that it's not so much a NASA rocket and more a space station, with all its components neatly docked together and the whole thing planted just south of Regent's Park. And she's begun to wonder if there's not some way of running giant cables between all the world's revolving restaurants, with little chairs hanging off them, like on the ski-lifts. In the Beautiful Decrepit Future this may be the only means of international travel: sitting in a plastic seat, creeping high above the silent cities, as the revolving restaurants are cranked by hand.

Queues of people will fill the stairs, all patiently waiting for their long, slow journeys. People will be too tired, too philosophical to fight. In the past, the curvature of the earth might have been an issue, but the height of these new skyscrapers should see to that.

As you creep through the cold, still air on your plastic seat you'll occasionally pass couples coming the other way. How're things in Budapest? you'll say. How many days' travel is it from here? And it'll be so good to see a fellow human you'll find yourself longing to reach out and touch them. But the closest they'll come to you will be fifty metres or so. You'll watch them slowly pass. Then you'll both carry on in different directions. And you'll keep on looking back over your shoulder, until they're just tiny specks of people, then finally gone.

Yukiko sleeps. She can't seem to help it. She only has to take a seat or stretch out on a hotel bed these days and she's out, like a boxer hitting the deck. And the next thing she's coming round, all weak and sickly, and even more exhausted than she was before. At night, in its allotted hours, her sleep is fitful, unproductive. She wonders if maybe some unidentified gland fails to spit the appropriate dose of something important into her bloodstream. Or perhaps it is the English air.

Of course, she's still burnt out after the last few months of college. Plus her internal clock has yet to align itself to UK Time. Then there was the flight itself. Twelve solid hours of inertia, breathing all that depleted air. Isn't there legislation, she thinks, that limits the number of years a flight attendant can work before they're grounded? Something happens. A thickening of the ankles, or constriction of the blood vessels in the brain. Then there were the late nights out with her sister before coming up here. Yuki doesn't usually drink that much, but everyone else seemed to be throwing it down their throats with such grim determination. Including her sister. Who never used to drink at all.

She opens her eyes and has a quick glance round the coach to see if anyone's noticed she was sleeping. Across the aisle, Mrs Kudo sits and stares out the window, watching the West Yorkshire moors roll by, apparently enthralled. Yuki's talked to her two or three times and found her to be perfectly pleasant. Her only problem is that, along with every other woman on the coach, she's a clear forty years Yuki's senior.

She checks her phone for messages, then opens up her notebook. She's kept a notebook since she was twelve – for her sketches, plus any odd little observations/hare-brained ideas. It is currently the place to note down anything idiosyncratically English. She is an anthropologist! For example, the tendency for English couples to argue in the street, regarding the most personal matters. Household finances . . . rumours of possible infidelities. Sure, they're *drunk*, but even so.

She is like Columbo, gathering evidence. Imagines herself in grubby grey macintosh shambling around the streets of England, taking it all in. She will be mocked, naturally. Oh, that scruffy, bumbling Japanese girl! So ignorant of local custom. What an utter buffoon. Until at last she shuffles on up to the blondest, best-dressed suspect (in the most prosaic possible surroundings – their kitchen, say, or the drive to their expensive-looking house) and with notebook open, slightly cross-eyed, she scratches her head and throws one hand up into the air. And with a few choice words reveals the inconsistencies in their story, their motive, along with some vital clue everybody else had missed. Then she shrugs and smiles that fractured smile as the uniformed cops head on in with their handcuffs and escort the guilty party out to the waiting car. Not so bumbling now, wouldn't you say!

This whole trip is, in fact, one super-big investigation. A mission of non-stop note-taking and forensic examination. Every inedible English meal is photographed pristine before her. She finishes a bar of chocolate and presses the wrapper like a leaf between the pages of her book. It may be nothing but the apparent exotica of a foreign culture. But there is also the conviction that with sufficient vigilance and chocolate bar wrappers there might emerge a real and profound appreciation. Which may in turn lead to some critical point when the Answer is revealed and suddenly it all makes sense to her – maybe months off into the future, when she's back in Japan.

To be honest, pretty much everything beyond the coach's window seems alien to Yuki. The quality of light . . . the little houses . . . the fields in between. Even the glass through which she stares appears to be manufactured to European specifications – the rubber mouldings that hold the glass in place. The fabric on the seat before her . . . its density of colour . . . the depth of the fabric's own fine fur. Even these tiny screws, Yuki thinks, at each corner of the plastic panel below the window are undeniably alien. You would never see a screw like that in Japan. And all at once she becomes conscious of the million individual parts that have come together in this coach's construction, and imagines each one slowly recalled to the place of its origin. She sees the screws begin to twist beneath the window. The plastic veneers peel away. Until suddenly the coach erupts into its near-infinite number of elements, which go twirling off and away to every part of the horizon. So that all that is left are the thirty-five Japanese travellers, their Tour Guide, Hana Kita, and Mr Thompson, their English Coach Driver. All thirty-seven of them standing on a moorland road, with their luggage stacked beside them, on a cold, grey English day.

*

Yukiko has been doing a fair amount of travelling lately. In her notebook somewhere she has made a list of all the tubes, trains, buses, taxis, etc. she's recently occupied – the many and varied capsules that have shunted her about the place. Naturally, air travel remains the most exhilarating/disorienting – the one with the most potential for transcendence. If Yukiko had her way airline passengers would be obliged to wear something Futuristic. Ideally, something designed in the 1950s for how they imagined the twenty-first century would be. One day, she tells herself, she will create a figure-hugging jumpsuit in orange rayon and wear it on a regular domestic flight, without any hint of irony. Just to see how people react.

If she hadn't been so busy studying Fashion, Yuki would very much have liked to train to be an Airport

Designer. She remains vaguely hopeful of someone approaching her regarding just such a position after coming across her sketches on the internet. If/when that happens she will just have to squeeze the extra work in at the weekends.

The fundamental mistake in airport design, Yuki believes, is that everything is so goddamned white. There is altogether too much light, both natural and artificial. The notion persists for some reason that, since the passengers are about to head skyward, a sense of space and whiteness is what's required, to get everyone in the mood. But Yuki considers this to be a grave, grave error. In truth, the airport customer is preparing for a period of confinement, in what is essentially a fast-moving tunnel. One's pre-flight, airport-bound hours are a process of surrender. We grow quiet. We withdraw into ourselves. And no wonder. We are about to pass through a portal. What's required, Yuki feels, is warm, dark spaces. Something womb-like. Airports should, in fact, be underground.

Another of Yuki's bugbears regarding modern-day airports – and one of the first things she will set about remedying once appointed – is having to travel the thirty or forty miles out to where the planes arrive/depart from the city after which the airport is named. Such a ridiculous waste of time. Yuki's plan is to create a new generation of airports situated directly below the world's major cities. Once the air traveller arrives at his/her destination and passes through immigration he/she will simply step into an elevator and, moments later, stride out into: the Champs-Elysées, Times Square, Sydney Harbour, or the lobby of whatever hotel they happen to be staying in.

Sure, this will entail a good deal of digging, but Yuki believes that people are willing to rise to a challenge, particularly one with such evident benefits. She's equally confident that there already exist large and noisy machines capable of doing the necessary earth-removal. If not, she is prepared to invent such a machine in any spare time she can conjure up between her regular job as a Leading Fashion House Designer and her weekend post creating a new generation of subterranean urban airports. She has already completed two or three rough sketches.

Most of the excavation will be spent creating the vast cavern necessary to house the airport. The tunnels/ corridors down which the aeroplanes will fly need not necessarily be that wide. Just big enough to accommodate a plane's typical wingspan, plus an extra metre or two. But oh, yes – quite, quite long. At the point of entry Yuki envisages a sort of slash in the earth, somewhere just beyond the city's perimeter. As the plane approaches its destination there is bound to be a little nervousness among the passengers. But people enjoy a tiny bit of nervousness now and again, don't you think? The captain's voice will come over the speakers: 'Ladies and gentlemen, we are now approaching London Scar. Please fasten your seat belts, super-tight.' Then – just imagine – dropping, dropping.

Peering out of the little windows to see the ground rising up to meet you. Children standing over their bicycles, open-mouthed. Then suddenly – POW! – the sky is gone, and the whole plane is swallowed up by Planet Earth and all you see are rocks and soil through the windows. And you are flying underground!

The coach starts to lurch and slow as it navigates the roads on the outskirts of a village. The passengers begin to look up. The chatter increases in tempo and volume. People are peering out in every direction. Yukiko thinks, If only there had been a Haworth International Airport. Imagine how much time and effort I could have saved myself over the last five days. Sure, I wouldn't have spent four days in London with the sister I hadn't seen in years. But I'd have been able to catch up with her later, most likely. Right now I'd be two hundred metres underground and heading for the elevator marked 'Brontë Parsonage'.

Way down at the front of the coach Hana Kita is talking into a microphone. People are leaning into the aisle and peering over headrests, but there's no sign of her. Hana Kita is pretty short but Yuki's guessing that the reason no one can see her is that she's making the announcement from her seat.

We're now arriving in Haworth, she says, which provokes even more twisting and turning and faces up against the windows. Well, of course we are, thinks Yukiko, you goddamned idiots. Why the hell else would we be pulling in here? But the crazy old women are determined to crank themselves right up. They have come all this way and are going to make damned sure they get excited about every last little thing.

As the coach pulls off the road and into some sort of car park Hana Kita runs through the itinerary, explaining how many hours they'll be spending in Haworth and how the coach must leave promptly at two thirty if they're to reach the hotel in Windermere in time to make themselves comfortable before the evening meal. She insists that it's quite safe to leave belongings on the coach, since Mr Thompson will be remaining with the vehicle at all times. And now everyone's looking over at the back of Mr Thompson's bald head as he continues to wrestle the coach into position – a head which, according to Hana Kita, is packed tight with the highest-quality trustworthiness.

Hana Kita continues to blather away and Mr Thompson is still heaving on his big old steering wheel, but already people are getting to their feet and pulling on coats and jackets. Eager to get out there and breathe in some authentic Brontë air. That's right, thinks Yuki. The same dreadful air that killed all three Brontë sisters when they were barely out of school.

She checks to make sure she has all her belongings and joins the others shuffling down the aisle. Then finally they're out into cold and damp West Yorkshire. Further, barely audible announcements are made by Hana Kita. She raises the handle of her rolled-up umbrella, like a periscope. Yukiko swings her rucksack up onto her shoulders and they all go marching into town.

Yukiko's first impression of Haworth is how very brown everything is – the walls, the roads, the buildings. London and Leeds had nothing like this level of brownness. Perhaps it is a moss of some sort, brought on by local industry. Or some rural, Northern mould.

The army of Japanese ladies stomps down the streets, with Yukiko at the rear, feeling unspeakably self-conscious. The same stomach-cramping embarrassment that gripped her in the hotel bar last night whilst everyone else sat around, chatting about their upcoming surgery . . . their son's promotion . . . the terrible pounding their pensions had taken in recent years – apparently oblivious. Yuki noticed the barman glance over on a couple of occasions, and how other guests would stroll into the bar and briefly freeze before this great mass of jibbering elderly Japs. Until eventually she had to creep away up to her room, to watch TV and sip whiskey straight from the bottle – hopping from channel to channel, hoping to find something stupid enough for her to understand.

She does her best now to keep her head down. Even if I were on my own, she thinks, and wearing my Jackie O sunglasses people would still pick up on my Japanese-ness. The hair. The skin, maybe. The way I walk.

Mrs Kudo comes striding up alongside her. Yuki sees how she glances at her packed-tight rucksack, then asks if she wasn't inclined to leave it on the coach. Yuki shakes her head. Explains how her actual suitcase got lost on the flight over. So now she must be super-cautious about her rucksack and insists on having it with her at all times.

And this is more or less true. Yukiko did indeed stand at the carousel at Heathrow for almost an hour, constantly expecting to see her case the very next moment, before it occurred to her that it might actually be somewhere else. So, having landed in Britain and been subjected to a most unpleasant interview regarding her visit, its purpose, duration, etc. – all in a language she barely understood – her next task was to fill out a form in the same strange language about her luggage, what was in it, its value, etc. and to offer an address to which it might

14

be forwarded if anyone happened to trip over it in the coming weeks.

Ever since, she has imagined her suitcase, forlorn, on any number of international airport carousels . . . or wedged in some corner of a plane's hold . . . lying on its side in the long grass at the airport's perimeter . . . and even falling silently through a clear blue sky.

The only possible upside to the loss of her suitcase is that it has provided Yuki with a solid justification for buying a whole new bunch of clothes. In fact, one of the revelations of her first few days in England has been the ubiquity of charity shops and the abundance of affordable, often perfectly eccentric items on their rails. Without doubt, Yuki's favourite purchase so far has been the pair of size five dress shoes that she estimates to be at least sixty years old and which must have once belonged either to a rather formal lady or to a man with tiny, tiny feet. She's also picked up two fifties-style print skirts and four blouses and admired various vintage pieces which, though she couldn't quite afford them herself, would cost a holy cow fortune back home.

Of course, she could simply fill a container with such items, ship the whole lot back to Japan and sell them, which would almost certainly net her a profit significant enough to set her up to do this full-time. Every two or three months she'd fly over to the UK, accompanied by her own small gang of fashion lackeys, and together they would make their way along every metre of rail in Oxfam, Scope and Age UK. But that is how Yukiko is these days. One minute she's quite convinced she'll actually go ahead and damn well do this. Is writing herself reminders to read up on the necessary certificates regarding taxes, shipping, etc. and becoming altogether quite breathless with excitement. Then, five minutes later, she's slumped in Kumiko's armchair, slowly losing consciousness, thinking it's just about the dumbest idea she's ever had.

Anyway, due to the cock-up with her luggage, half the clothes she's currently wearing and most of those crammed into her rucksack belong to her sister, not least the New Balance trainers, which are a size too big and only stay on her feet due to the fact that she's wearing an extra pair of socks. Frustratingly, Yuki had to go out and buy a new phone charger, after specifically acquiring and packing the little fitting that would enable her to use her own charger in the west. The new UK charger appears to work – has already charged Yuki's phone on two occasions. But she remains sceptical, as if the power on which it now runs is thin and capricious and may at any point simply drain away into the air.

So Yukiko heads on into Haworth, in her too-big trainers, with Mrs Kudo marching alongside her, being deeply sympathetic about her luggage-loss. The same thing has happened to her, she says. She knows how unsettling it is. In fact, says Mrs K, when the Brontës' mother originally moved to Haworth from faraway Cornwall, her luggage came along independently by ship. But the ship was wrecked and she lost all her personal possessions. So arrival in Haworth after suffering comprehensive and troubling luggage-loss is a time-honoured thing.

Yukiko stops, right there in the middle of the street, obliging Mrs Kudo to stop beside her. Yuki looks her square in the eye; insists on clarification. Well, says Mrs K, they may have managed to fish one or two books out of the water. There is a mention somewhere of the sisters reading a book after their mother had died and the pages being stained with seawater. But everything else was lost.

And as they walk on again, Yuki wonders what sort of state she'd be in now if she hadn't packed all her most precious belongings – specifically, her mother's clothes and photos – in her hand luggage. Well, the fact is, of course, that she would simply have expired. Or exploded, like the coach, into a million pieces. The emergency services would've turned up, but some old fellow who'd seen the whole thing would say, 'Don't even bother with a bin bag. That Japanese girl was so upset she just went up in a puff of bloody steam.'

Well, Haworth sure must be super-small because about five minutes after leaving the coach Hana Kita's rolled-up brolly is turning up a cobbled alley. And right there is some grey old church and graveyard, with the parsonage looming up beyond. The moment they lay eyes on it the ladies all let out tiny squeals and whimpers, as if they've arrived at some magical kingdom where all their pains and aches will be soothed away.

Yuki was under the impression the Brontë girls had been raised in uncompromising squalor, with much soot and scarce little soap, but it's a fair-sized house. Having said that, it doesn't look the least bit welcoming. In fact, it looks about as miserable as it's possible for a building to be. They all troop through a side-gate, up half a dozen or so steps and out onto a little patio, then head straight on up to the front door, everyone gawping all around and taking in every detail. But before she's reached the door Yuki senses that there's a problem. The ladies ahead of her begin to bunch up. There is a blockage of some sort. And it slowly becomes apparent that the parsonage is actually closed.

Yuki thinks, Well, this could easily turn quite nasty.

Some of these women are pretty nuts. We come all this way and we're refused entry? Then we're just gonna have to chop down one of those old trees in the graveyard and use it as a battering ram.

But Hana Kita has fluttered up onto the toppermost step and is waving her rolled-up brolly. Everything is perfectly fine, she says. We are just a single, solitary minute early. An oversight brought about by over-keenness to get here and look about. A murmur of something like reassurance sweeps through the crowd. OK, so maybe we'll hold back on all the rioting and looting for a couple of minutes. But despite her tidy little smile you can see how much this pains poor Hana Kita. How much she is sickened by this indelible blemish on her name.

So the ladies stand around and glare at the main door, as if working on it telekinetically. And now that she has a little time Yuki is finding that she has precisely *no* desire to head on into this weird old house. That she would, in fact, be very happy for the door to remain locked all day.

She thinks that maybe when everyone else goes in she might just slip away to some quiet little corner of the gardens. Where people might be less inclined to ask why she doesn't join in. Or the graveyard. Yes, a graveyard would be a good place to hide.

She's beginning to wonder if this whole trip was such a great idea. Whether it isn't simply going to be too upsetting. And she's digging her hands deep into her pockets, getting more and more anxious, when her eyes settle on one of the windows a couple of metres away and

19

she realises that she *knows* one particular corner of this intersection of stone sill, wall, glass and painted frame. She has seen it – *studied* it – a hundred times. It is in the background to one of her mother's Five Photographs. In her rucksack she has a photo of her mother standing at this very spot. Her mother standing right here, before her, with the sun in her eyes – kind and beautiful and not at all dead.

Well, that's really given her something to chew on. How, she wonders, do I feel about *that*. For some reason, Yuki had assumed that, like the other four photographs – outside the hotel . . . in her room . . . the tree . . . the water – that particular shot had been taken somewhere else. Some public house maybe, away down the cobbled hill. The parsonage, she'd always imagined, would be kind of white.

She's still standing there, busy transplanting her mother from some other unspecified location to the space before her, when the main door opens. Hana Kita makes another brief announcement, and before she's finished that great horde of ageing Japanese ladies starts shuffling forward, like cattle, on into the old, old house.

Yukiko thinks, Well, OK. It all makes sense again. This is why I'm here. And she vows to return to this spot, to have a better look, before the day is out. Picks up her bag and heads on in.

A woman at a small desk smiles meekly at each person who files past her. As if to say, Welcome, women of all ages and nationalities. Welcome, fellow Brontë lovers.

Yuki is inclined to confide in her that she is not like all these crazies she's been lumped together with since the previous evening. Is not here to bow deeply before some long-dead sisters and their dull old books. Wants to whisper, I'm actually a *detective*. Like Columbo. Here on business. But, before she's halfway down the hall, there's some fuss regarding her rucksack. It hadn't occurred to her that she might not be able to take it all the way round the house with her. She's not 100% sure exactly what the concern is. That she might knock some precious Brontë ornament off a shelf and smash it? Or maybe attempt to slip some little relic into her overstuffed rucksack and set up her own modest Brontë Museum back home?

After some discussion between herself and a member of staff with Mrs Kudo acting as intermediary the situation is made plain. No bags in the house. And Yuki is obliged to head on back to a large cupboard by the front door and to relinquish it. In exchange she receives a pink numbered ticket. OK, she says (see how her English improves with every second), then is finally allowed to go on into the house. But she feels deeply uncomfortable now. Is convinced that when the lady in charge of bag-security is next engaged in English chit-chat, or goes off to make an English cup of tea, someone will creep in and grab her rucksack and make off with all her priceless, private things.

She does her very best not to think about it. Instead, she thinks on the fact that, considering how big the house appears from the outside, the rooms are actually pretty small. Half of that first room is roped off, presumably to stop people sitting on chairs that once had a Brontë sitting in them or at desks where they scratched away at some gloomy Brontë book.

Yukiko is beginning to feel pretty agitated. Can't stop thinking about the many very important things in her rucksack and how she'd pretty much die without them. Being all penned in with the aged ladies in this half-roped-off little room isn't helping. Oh no, indeed.

Hana Kita is dispensing great slabs of Brontë Wisdom, regarding whose study this was and what kind of studious things used to go on here. Yukiko, like Hana Kita, is on the short side, so has no hope of seeing her face. But the woman's voice is so hushed and hallowed she can barely make out half of what she says.

Yukiko can tell when she's in trouble: she digs her thumbnail into the top of her forefinger, or the nail of her forefinger into the flesh of her thumb. She does this, she knows, when she's anxious, frustrated or embarrassed. It's not as if she makes a conscious decision to start digging the nail of one digit into another. She just looks down and there it is. Could it be, she has wondered, that by bringing about a small but powerful charge of actual pain she is trying to find expression for some deeper pain that is only half-formed and unintelligible? All she knows is that it is a guaranteed symptom of the fact that something ugly's bubbling away, which is certainly the case right now. Because she's digging the hell out of her forefinger with her thumbnail – practically drawing blood. Also getting quite breathless. Poor Yuki is huffing and puffing like she's just run up a hill.

She manages to hang on for another few seconds, then finally turns and bundles her way out of the room. And long before she reaches the bag department she has that little pink ticket in her hand. I need a puff on my inhaler, she tells herself, which is in the top pocket of my rucksack. Otherwise, I may well just completely fade away.

She zips right by the woman on the ticket desk. Lifts a forefinger, as if to say, I will be just one single minute. Or even, I'm digging the nail of my thumb into my forefinger. And we all know what that means.

She hands her ticket over to the Bag Lady, who looks back at her in a state of wizened bewilderment. Then at last Yuki has her bag and is heading for the door, out into the cold North English air. Plucking out her puffer, giving it a vigorous little shake. Exhaling as far as she can, in order to squeeze every last bit of breath right out of her. Then plugging the puffer in her mouth, releasing the gas and sucking it up, up, up. Holding the medication right there, locked up inside her, so she can absorb every atom of its chemical goodness.

Yuki had two brand-new, boxed-up puffers in her bag that went missing, along with her clothes, toiletries, phone charger, etc. Fortunately, she also had one open in her jacket pocket, in case she needed it during the flight, but with no more than a couple of days' puffs left in it. So on her first morning in the UK she had to make an appointment with Kumiko's doctor and got a prescription for two replacement puffers.

Sometimes when she fills herself right up and holds it there she has this idea of herself as being completely empty, like a human balloon. She once read somewhere that every cell of a human being is 97% space, so maybe that's not too far from the truth. Right now, her biggest concern is that the puffer she got from the UK doctor isn't perhaps half as potent as the ones she gets back home and that there may come a moment in the near future when, without warning, the puffer will fail to deliver the necessary fix. That she'll suddenly find herself gasping and flailing in a foreign country, with neither the breath nor even the charge on her phone to call for help.

A pair of bona fide Brontë Lovers stroll by, heading for the main door, and glance at Yuki bent over her rucksack. She smiles pathetically back at them. Then, once they've gone she has another look at the front of the parsonage, as her breath settles. Specifically, at the spot where her mother stood. She opens up the top of her rucksack, pulls out a thick brown envelope. Tips out a smaller envelope, with five colour photographs in it, and flicks through them until she finds the one taken here ten years earlier.

Yuki's mother looks straight at the camera, almost smiling. Yukiko tries to gauge how far from the wall she must have stood. Not very far at all. She gets to her feet, moves slowly towards the parsonage and, by referring repeatedly to the photograph, finds the right place. She turns, drops her hand and, for a moment, looks forward, imagining her mother's lovely face. Her mother's face with a smile just beginning to form there, the same as every photograph ever taken of her.

A couple of minutes later Yukiko tucks her puffer and photographs into her jacket pocket and heads back into the parsonage. Raises the self-same finger she was waving in the air when she ran out, but now points it down the hallway, like a lady's pistol. I'm with the crazy Japanese Elders, the finger says – and they let her go right on in.

She hands her rucksack over to the Bag Lady a second time, then joins the women as they squeeze into another of the downstairs rooms. Hana Kita is talking about the Brontës' father and how he once took a pair of scissors to one of his daughters' dresses for being too colourful, and how, when he was in a bad mood, he'd take his gun out the back and fire a couple of shots off into the sky. Hana Kita delivers these little anecdotes as if this is charming, old-fashioned English behaviour, but Yuki is fast coming to the conclusion that Papa Brontë was a complete and utter nut. So, in order to avoid hearing any more such nonsense, she slips away again from the Elders and goes drifting in and out of the rooms on her own, happy to simply stare at the furniture and Brontë knick-knacks in her own, slightly mystified way.

But the Parsonage Ladies must have had an eye on her, because pretty soon one of them comes tiptoeing over and taps Yukiko on the shoulder. Yuki's sure she's committed some dreadful indiscretion – that she has touched something that must not be touched. But the Parsonage Lady slips into her hand a small blue leaflet, then creeps off back down the hall. Is gone before Yuki appreciates that the leaflet contains a paragraph in Japanese relating to each room of the house. And she really is quite touched by this. Especially considering how much running in and out she's done.

In one room there's a little sofa, upon which, according to the leaflet, poor Emily died. No doubt back then a sofa would have cost a great deal of money, but Yuki's pretty sure that if anyone died on one of her sofas – and particularly from some Victorian fever – the first thing she'd do is drag it out the back and have herself a sofa-bonfire. But in the Brontës' day, apparently, they just wiped it down and maybe opened the window to air the room for a couple of hours. It's almost admirable, but Yuki feels the English sure do seem to like to hold onto things beyond the point when they cease to be practical. In Japan, an old house like this would've been flattened and rebuilt half a dozen times, along with every other building in town. It seems quite perverse that British streets are still packed with creaky old buildings, with their dark little rooms, their ancient glass still rattling in their windows and their odd little chimney pots perched on their pointy little roofs.

She pops her head into a bare-looking kitchen and has a little wander round it. Here, she reads, Emily would sometimes make bread with her right hand while holding a book of German verse in her left. Well, OK, Yuki thinks, now you're talking. Because she applauds any woman who is unashamed of her intelligence. Also, what a great little trick. Over dinner last night the Elders were discussing Branwell, the dissolute Brontë brother, and someone mentioned a little party-piece he was said to have performed at the local pub in which he'd write a line of Latin with his right hand while writing the same thing in Greek with his left. So now Yuki's wondering if the Brontë kids weren't, in fact, exceptionally gifted linguists – or whether having your hands do different things simultaneously wasn't just about as wild an evening as you were likely to have back then.

She heads up the stairs, where it's a little cooler – and more dismal, if that's possible – and stands on the landing, consulting her leaflet, where she learns that there were, in fact, another two Brontë girls, who died when they were still children. Two invisible, extra Brontës no one's ever heard of, since neither lived long enough to lift a pen. The first bedroom she enters, it seems, is where the mother passed away, knowing that all her children would have to go on, motherless. With just their crazy father to look after them. And this really is just about too much for poor Yukiko. She's tempted to throw herself onto the old bed and have a good long cry about it, and might have done so if she didn't suspect that the bed, bedroom floor and the entire Brontë house would likely collapse around her, which would only mean her being dragged off to the local jailhouse, to be beaten about the body with copies of *Wuthering Heights*.

And suddenly Yukiko has had enough of death and child-abandonment, and slips quickly and quietly from room to room, like a ghost, until she encounters a large glass cabinet which holds one of Charlotte's old dresses – faded pink, with traces of what appears to be some sort of paisley print. The waistline impossibly narrow. And, more than most, Yukiko appreciates how much work would have gone into the making of that tiny dress. The hundred individual pleats, gathered under the waistband. All the folds and stitching at the neck. Yuki suddenly can't get enough of this dress. The waist, hardly wider than the neckline; the dress's very headlessness. She stands and studies the thing until the glass case begins to slowly spin, the top floats free and the dress gradually emerges, like a satellite being delivered into space. And the dress floats off around the room, out onto the landing and all around the house.

Yuki walks on down a different staircase and is in sight of the gift shop, making her way between glass cabinets containing various Brontë personal items. She doesn't intend to spend more than a minute or two here – is already looking forward to getting out into the daylight – but one of the first things she spots is a lock of hair, said to be Charlotte's. And, weirdly, this makes Charlotte powerfully real to Yuki. A living, breathing woman. Then a handful of children's toys that must have belonged to the infant Brontës and which, her leaflet tells her, were discovered beneath the floorboards. But what really knocks Yuki out are the scraps of paper covered in crayoned drawings and the tiniest handwriting. It takes her a moment or two to work out that they are, in fact, miniature, home-made books. Stitched and written with a child's determined hand.

She's still standing, staring at them, with her face so close to the glass she can feel its coldness, when Mrs Kudo joins her. Yukiko knows that she's there. Knows that it will be Mrs Kudo. And without even turning to her, says, Aren't they just about the most beautiful things you've ever seen?

For two or three years now Yuki has been collecting children's books about Space Travel – ideally, from the Sixties and early Seventies, though she's not averse to earlier publications which contain a little less science and a lot more speculation, with drawings of rockets that look as if they're made of concrete, and moon stations with massive windows where astro-folk can relax and read a book.

Yuki's convinced she'd make a pretty good astronaut. She's patient, capable of medium-length periods of concentration and, despite all the panic regarding the loss of her puffers and phone charger, is really quite laid-back. She's not sure she'd want to sign up for a trip to, say, Jupiter, but is confident she'd be able to handle four or five days' floating about, just outside the stratosphere. Carrying out repairs on a space station, say. Or collecting samples. Or blowing up some meteor that was heading our way.

The whole weightlessness thing is one of the main attractions – just as it is, she suspects, for professional astronauts (though they'd never admit to it). So it's perfectly natural that when you first get up there you're going to goof about, tossing pens to pals, flipping up peanuts and chomping them out of the air, etc. But pretty soon you'd be only too happy to get on with some serious experiments, whatever they might be. Yuki thinks the lack of gravity might help with her sleeping. In space all your muscles and bones have no option but to just sort of hang there. Which must be weird to begin with, but you hear about astronauts returning to earth several centimetres taller than when they climbed into their rocket, and your body has got to appreciate that. So Yuki wouldn't be at all surprised if, at the close of day, when she zips herself into her pod or secures herself to the wall with Velcro, she sleeps like a top.

Part of the deal in her agreeing to be an astronaut would be that she got to design the crew's clothes. Not the shiny suits you wear when taking off and landing, which she imagines have to be made of fireproof material with special wires for microphone cables and so on, but the kind of outfit you change into once you've cleared the earth's gravity and are just floating around. The basic design would have to be clean and simple. No collars or cuffs which might get caught on important levers. Plus, it would be good to avoid beige, which has long been a cliché in casual spacewear. You could have a different outfit for each day. That way, when you look around and see how everyone's wearing blue with yellow trim you know it must be Wednesday. Or if everyone's in a pink jumpsuit with a Fifties V-neck you know that it's Friday and there's only one more day to go.

*

Of course, The Future won't last forever. At least, not in the shiny, bright way we've come to imagine it. The day will surely dawn when the systems fail, the teetering tower of our technically dependant existence topples and everything suddenly slows, slows, slows right down.

If you happen to be on a flight at that particular juncture your best hope is that the plane will simply glide towards the nearest airport or flattish-looking field. And wherever that happens to be is where you'll likely stay, quite possibly for ever. Unless you feel like walking the twelve thousand kilometres home. Or cycling. If you happen to have a bicycle.

All the tankers will slowly find themselves beached and picked apart by barefoot infants. The office blocks will be turned into glasshouses. We will live modestly, with modest aspirations. We will do our best to embrace our new slow life. But Yuki doesn't regard all this as unbearably awful. True enough, there will be a period of adjustment – a period that may last some time. But once everything is settled we'll be able to appreciate our new circumstances. Clean air! And imagine the silence! In no time at all the weeds will sweep through the malls and gas stations, and the moss will get to work. The world will become handsomely dilapidated. Yuki imagines us advancing courageously into this Beautiful Decrepit Future. Or, if not with courage, then innocence.

Yuki and the Elders are hiking up onto the moors, to see the heather. The heather which, Hana Kita has told them, is quite exquisite when it's in flower. When she brings her groups up here in late summer, she says, they sit in its midst and eat their lunch like some purple heather *hanami*. But right now the sky is heavy and the heather's like old grey string, as if this place was once the bed of some ancient ocean from which the sea retreated centuries ago.

But they must hike out here in order that the Elders can see where the Brontës used to go when taking a break from novel-writing. To view their natural habitat. There is talk of an old wreck of a house, way out on the moors, which is said to figure in *Wuthering Heights*. Though it's not clear what they're meant to do when they get there, except gaze in wonder, turn around and hike all the way back to town.

Some of the Elders are pretty fit, and desperate to prove it by going stomp, stomp, stomp off towards the hilltop in their brand-new boots, while those Elders who aren't so able do their damnedest to keep up, even if it means bringing on a coronary. Yuki couldn't care less.

Her rucksack weighs a ton and her feet are slipping and sliding in Kumi's too-big trainers. Which, by the way, are starting to get a little scuffed around the toes. And Kumiko is not the kind of person to overlook a little scuffing. She's the kind of person who will mind a very great deal.

After a while they drop on down into some sort of hollow, along a path in which the stones are polished from all the boots that have marched over them. Yuki wonders how many Brontë fans must tramp up and down this way each year. Entire Brontë-loving armies. And how many really have the first idea what it is they're looking for?

The Elders congregate in the bottom of the little valley and by the time Yuki joins them they're hovering round some big old rock which is as smooth and polished as the stones in the path. Everyone quietens down, then Hana Kita declares that the Brontë sisters would often sit here when they were out walking. So this old lump of rock has been accorded some crazy name, such as Brontë Rock . . . the Brontë Chair . . . or Brontë Something. Yuki can't quite make it out. But now the Elders all stare at the rock most gravely, as if they can imagine how the Brontë girls once perched upon it. Then one of them reaches out and strokes the hallowed old thing, as if it's some petrified moorland creature. Which, of course, just encourages all the rest to do the same.

As the Elders pat the rock Yuki stands and watches, thinking, Do all women go soft as they grow old? Or just the ones who read the Brontës? It's a rock. Just a big old rock. And if the rock does, in fact, lend itself to being sat on, then why would it only be the Brontës doing the sitting? Wouldn't everyone else who came along have the same idea? It's as if, in the Brontë-lovers' soft heads, these moors were empty, save the occasional wandering Brontë. Not another living creature dared enter their realm.

She really doesn't know why she gets so wound up about such things. In principle, she has no grudge against the sisters. Plus, having seen Charlotte's dress and the little books she and her sisters made with their own small hands they now seem to have really existed in a way that they hadn't before. When they were girls, Yuki and Kumiko used to make their own little books. Would devote entire weekends to cutting them up and filling the pages with tiny writing. Like sacred texts from some shrunken world.

Now everyone follows Hana Kita over to a stream and the simple bridge across it – just a couple of heavy stone slabs dropped into place. A pretty enough spot, but within a minute it has been revealed as being Brontë Bridge. Where the girls would sit and dangle their feet and stare into the water. Imagine! The Brontë sisters sitting and staring into the water and thinking about their books.

And not for the first time today, Yuki thinks, Is it not possible that the Brontës led a thrilling secret existence? A life that didn't simply involve them wandering the moors, scraping away at their novels before expiring, one by one, on some poorly stuffed sofa. Is it not conceivable that they might have got up to something a little more wayward, once the sun went down? Might they not on occasion have got so thoroughly sick of all the awful silence and their own graceful suffering that they crept into their father's room while he slept, took his pistol and slipped out onto the moors with it? That they covered their faces with what was left of the dresses he'd attacked with the scissors and held up some passing carriage. Before running off, all three of them, whooping and cackling, into the darkness, with fistfuls of jewellery stuffed into their pockets and bank notes blowing across the windy moors.

They'd need a stolen horse or two on which to charge across the heather and carry them back to town, to the local alehouse, where they'd spend the rest of the night puffing on pipes and drinking, along with a good deal more whooping and cackling. And when a fellow-drinker asked if they'd care to try and write Greek with one hand and Latin with the other they'd come over all bristly and pull out their father's gun again, and say that they weren't here to write goddamned Greek or goddamned Latin, either Individually or At the Same Goddamned Time. They were here to drink and smoke, and to spit on the floor if they wanted. Then everyone would back off and the sisters would go back to talking too loud and shrieking and drinking. And maybe even a little singing. Songs about a gang of carefree young women who abandoned book-writing because it was too mind-numbingly dull when put alongside being highwaywomen and teaching rich ladies and gentlemen not to carry so much cash and jewellery with them whilst travelling in the wilder regions of the land.

Yukiko wonders if the occasional thrill might not have helped them live a little longer. Might not have put some heat into their cold young bones. Despite the risk of somebody one day pulling out a gun of their own and blowing out their pretty Brontë brains.

*

Another mile or so up the path they stop for lunch – a location with which Hana Kita is clearly familiar, judging by the way she casually encourages everyone to take a seat on the crop of low boulders. Yuki is tempted to enquire whether this collection of rocks doesn't also have its own significance in Brontëland. Was this not, perhaps, Brontë Picnic Corner? Or Brontë Quick Stop for a Pee? It's not as if Hana Kita should take sole responsibility for all this Brontë-nonsense. Then again, she's hardly helping put a stop to it.

Hana Kita instructs everybody to take out the lunch box they were handed in the hotel lobby this morning. In her own cardboard box Yuki finds an egg mayonnaise sandwich, a packet of crisps, a carton of juice and a Penguin biscuit. She places all four items on the ground, lined up squarely, and takes a photograph on her phone.

Most of the Elders are too busy with their own lunch to notice. The ones that do don't seem to mind. Perhaps they're getting used to it. Think, Oh, she's the girl who photographed her breakfast this morning. That's just the kind of thing young people do these days.

Women of the Elders' generation are forever complaining about how the Western bread-shops are ruining Japan's high streets but none of them seems to be making much of a fuss right now. True, one or two are alternating mouthfuls of English sandwich with bites of Japanese pickle – jars of which they've brought all these thousands of miles for this very purpose. But at least the crazy chatter has died down a bit.

Yuki gets to her feet and heads on over to the plastic bag which Hana Kita has designated as the Communal Garbage Receptacle and drops her sandwich wrapper in it. Then, rather than head back to her own little rock, she looks out over the moors for a couple of seconds, as if admiring the view, before ambling over to where Mrs Kudo sits.

Mrs K looks up and smiles as Yuki joins her. She asks Yuki what she made of the parsonage. They talk about what a weird old place it is. Then Yuki admits she wasn't expecting to enjoy her visit, but that in some ways – what with the dress, the handmade books, etc. – she finds it's made quite an impression on her.

For a little while they sit and eat together. Yuki wants to ask Mrs Kudo about her love of the Brontës. To get some idea what it is about the Brontës and women her age. But by the time she finally opens her mouth she's over-thought it all to such a degree that she asks Mrs Kudo *why* she loves the Brontë books, which is not what she meant at all. All the same, after some consideration Mrs Kudo turns to Yukiko and says that she loves the Brontë books for all sorts of reasons. But she first read them when she was quite young. Much younger than Yukiko is now. So her affection for the books is all mixed up with her own childhood and it would be hard to pick the two apart.

Again, Mrs Kudo and Yuki sit and eat in thoughtful silence, until Yukiko asks if there's one particular Brontë book Mrs Kudo loves above the rest. Without hesitation, Mrs Kudo leans in – leans right on in so that Yuki can feel her shoulder pressing against her own. *Jane Eyre*, she whispers. *Jane Eyre* is by far the best book to come out of that parsonage. She sits back and smiles, as if this has been proven. As if it is simply a matter of fact.

And in that instant Yuki thinks that she really must read *Jane Eyre* at the soonest opportunity – and quite possibly every other piece of writing created by a Brontë girl. She thinks she should maybe keep an online journal as she reads them. It could be a Major Project for the next year or so, or however long it takes. She can't believe she hasn't come up with this idea earlier. And in that very moment she also commits to persevering with her English, so that she might one day read the books in their original language – or at least *Jane Eyre*. Which is, of course, the finest Brontë book of all.

40

Then she thinks, This is how it starts. One minute you're eating some peculiar English sandwich. Someone whispers something in your ear and the next thing you know you've been infected with the Brontë Sickness. Worst of all, you actually welcome it. Despite the fact that, given time, it will destroy every last healthy cell.

Mrs Kudo brushes the crumbs from her hands and turns to Yuki. And Yuki just knows she's going to ask her which is her own personal favourite Brontë novel – and that when she discovers what a phony Yuki is, Brontë-wise, she will be so disappointed and look at her in such a sorry fashion that the small warm feeling she currently has inside her will be snuffed right out.

But, in fact, Mrs Kudo asks only if Yuki has recently graduated from college. Maybe it's just that she's about the right age. Yukiko nods. Mrs Kudo asks if she worked hard. Yuki nods again. Mrs K says she can tell. She says that her parents must be very proud of her.

Yukiko finds she can't speak. She can hardly swallow. She stares at the ground and sort of shrugs. But Mrs Kudo leans over, so that her shoulder touches Yuki's again, and says that she knows – knows for sure how very proud they must be.

After lunch, when everyone is filled right up with egg and bread, and all the litter is cleared away, someone suggests they should take a group photo. And suddenly Hana Kita is on her feet and striding around excitedly, corralling everyone into a tight little knot. There's quite a fuss regarding who might actually hold the camera and therefore not feature in the photo. Hana Kita announces that she should be the photographer, but people object vociferously, distraught at the very idea. Yukiko's pretty sure that the offer was 100% disingenuous. That Hana Kita is, in fact, determined to be right at the centre of the photographs – the fixed point around which this whole trip has been formed.

There's talk of tripods and the setting of timers. There is more fussing. Until Yukiko finally announces that *she* will take the photos. And when a couple of women protest, Yukiko insists with such force that the women are silenced, and almost inclined to take offence. But, one by one, they hand their cameras over to Yukiko. Rather the weird young girl, they're surely thinking, who never felt like one of the party anyway, than the graceful and much admired Hana Kita. And it is only as Yukiko is taking the third or fourth photograph that it occurs to her why perhaps she is so keen not to appear in the photographs herself. That she is not in fact here – at least, not in any way that she wishes to be recorded. That the whole aim of the enterprise is for her to creep in and go about her business almost silently and to leave no trace.

*

Within ten minutes everyone's heading back towards the hilltop, supposedly fortified, but in truth growing weary of this moor, the disappointing heather, the dismal weather. Some members of the party might even have asked Hana Kita how much more marching is needed in order to reach the ancient cottage – the place which may or may not have featured in a Brontë novel – if it didn't risk displaying a lack of gumption, or appear to diminish their love of the Brontë Girls.

Thankfully, after a few hundred yards one of the Elders suddenly stops in her tracks. Looks up at the sky and holds her hand out. And now the whole group is faltering, dissipating, looking about the place. Without a word, backpacks are removed, waterproof jackets are unfurled and hoods pulled up over heads – while Yuki watches. Mrs Kudo's close by and after pulling on her own raincoat she asks Yuki if she hasn't at least got a hat. Yuki shrugs and shakes her head. Mrs Kudo roots about in a pocket and produces what appears to be a solid but pliable block of plastic. She gives it a single sharp shake, the folded pleats flap open, like an accordion, and it reveals itself to be a plastic headscarf.

Yukiko stares down at it, disgusted. But Mrs Kudo presses it into her hand. Yuki doesn't even like the feel of it. She carries on standing there, with it hanging from her fingers, until finally Mrs Kudo tells her, quite forthrightly, that the only person who cares what she actually looks like is *her*. And since she won't be able to see what she looks like, then really, what is there to worry about?

There's a long, long pause before Yukiko finally succumbs and lifts it up to her head. Mrs Kudo turns away and finds something else with which to occupy herself, but once everyone is preparing to move off again, she glances over at Yukiko. Then laughs so hard she has to rest her hands on her knees to stop herself falling over. At such a hat. Such a hat with such a serious young woman under it.

*

And now the party has become faceless, anonymous. Nothing but a shiny great mass of colourful jackets with the raindrops rattling upon them, and the swish-swish of waterproofed arms and legs. It seems they still intend to reach the cottage – to lay their hands on it. Until the wind picks up and the rainfall suddenly intensifies. Then Hana Kita looks up at the sky. If there was just a single gap in the clouds, she thinks. Or a little light, out on the horizon. But the sky is dark and solid, and as she blinks in the rain she sees how several of the women have stopped and are squinting over at her. As if they're thinking, Is there no part of the Brontë Experience from which we might be spared?

She considers asking the Ladies for their opinion. Of instigating some brief debate. But when she opens her mouth she hears herself announce instead that their attempt at reaching the old wreck of a cottage is now officially abandoned. So that, in an instant, the slow trudge up the hill is transformed into a gleeful race back down it. And everyone goes scurrying down the path over the shiny wet stones at such speed that Hana Kita worries someone might slip and break an aged arm or leg. And that they'll be calling for helicopters to winch them out of here.

*

They make steady progress through the heather and soon are marching back across the Ancient Bridge of Brontë, curtseying by the Brontë Perching Rock before finally sensing again the presence of Brontë Museum Town in the valley below. Almost imperceptibly, Yuki slows her pace, allowing the other walkers to overtake her. The Elders must be thinking, Ha! These youngsters have no spunk! Can barely lift their little legs.

The rain continues. In the distance a wooden stile bridges the stone wall and Yuki decides that this will be her point of departure so she applies one final little bout of foot-dragging to ensure she's right at the back of the group by the time they reach it.

Just ahead of her, two Elders stride along, chatting. Yuki slows right down – watches them climb the steps and make their way over, then approaches the stile herself. She climbs the first couple of steps, then stands and watches the tour group push on into the drizzle, including kind Mrs Kudo. Then hops back down from the steps.

She shuffles along the wet wall, head down. Tries to find a crack among the stones to have another peek, without success. So she turns and crouches at the base of the wall, with her rucksack in her lap and her arms wrapped around it and that stupid plastic headscarf still on her head. She looks back up at the open moor, which suddenly feels unbearably wide and empty.

By her estimates she can endure maybe half an hour out here without slipping into a coma. Then a slow, slow walk back into town – with maybe another half an hour or so wandering round the not-so-pretty parts of the village which the tourists tend not to frequent.

She studies the toes of her sister's trainers, which she took without asking. Kumiko is almost certainly going to kill her. The most sensible option would be to simply dispose of them. Just stuff them in some litter bin and claim complete ignorance. Look her straight in the eye and say, I have no idea what the hell you're talking about.

Yukiko looks around. A piece of stone jutting out from the wall by her face is trimmed with white lichen, all curled and crimped like lace. She reaches up and nips it between finger and thumb. Carefully lifts and peels it away. She could maybe use it to trim the neckline of some weird, Brontë-era dress. The whole thing made from woven heather, moss, grass, etc. Natural things. And she'd wear it, to the shops – or just sit on a bus in it, as if it was the most normal thing in the world.

Despite it being cold and wet she's getting strangely sleepy. Back home somewhere she has two or three preliminary sketches for a sort of Invisibility Sleep Cape. For those occasions when one wishes to sleep in public. She sometimes convinces herself of its incredible potential and how mind-bendingly wealthy it could make her, but keeps getting stuck on the 'invisibility' element.

More recently, she's devoted some energy to a tiny tent you erect around your head and shoulders. You'll still be visible, but the people around you – on the tube/bus/park bench, etc. – will know to leave you alone. The tent will provide that all-important privacy that allows you to sleep without embarrassment. Not so much a Cape of Invisibility; more a Personal Urban Sleep Tent.

She checks the time. She thinks about her mother. About how she too must have walked across these same strange moors, in the company of women not that different from the ones with whom Yuki has spent the last twenty-four hours. And not for the first time, Yuki wonders whether it might be possible to grow so tired – so profoundly, debilitatingly drained and exhausted – that the dead finally come alive to you.

After a while she thinks that this may be a good time to have a little puff on her pipe. To help with her thinking. So she opens up her bag and starts rooting around for it.

The whole pipe-smoking thing kicked off the day she landed. She and Kumi were in a coffee shop on the King's Road when this big, bald guy went thundering past the window with a battered briefcase swinging in one hand and a lit pipe clamped between his teeth. It would've been good to know where he was heading in such a hurry. To deliver a lecture, maybe? Or late for some extramarital rendezvous? All Yuki saw was a big, bald guy in a winter coat, puffing down the pavement like a steam train. It was a most impressive sight.

Two days later she was on the top deck of a bus and noticed a man across the aisle, fiddling and fussing with a pipe of his own. Scraping at the bowl with the clean end of a matchstick, pulling the whole thing apart to suck and blow through the various components and bringing the stem up to his eye to see what was going on down there. When he was done and had put the bits back together he gave the bowl two or three sharp taps against the heel of his shoe, slipped it into an inside pocket and headed down the stairs. Yuki thought to herself, Well, that looks kind of fun.

That evening she mentioned her interest in English pipe-smoking to a friend of Kumi's, who told her about this shop that sells nothing but pipes, pipe tobacco and the little tools and knives you need to keep them clean. Yuki went out and found it the following morning. You couldn't really miss it. The window was full of pipe holders, pipes, fancy lighters, with a row of ceramic bowls below, each heaped with tobacco, as if some tiny ship had just stopped by and hauled the different tobaccos up from its hold with its own tiny crane.

Before she went in she thought, If anyone asks me, I'm buying a pipe for my dad, back home. But the shopkeeper didn't seem particularly bothered at having a young Japanese woman about the place and Yuki slowly made her way around, studying all the pipes and lighters and tobacco pouches in their little wooden cabinets, as if she was at the National Gallery, till she found herself at the counter.

About thirty pipes were laid out under the glass. Some had steel stems, some had wooden stems that were kind of curly. The bowls were made from all different coloured wood. The shopkeeper asked if she'd like him to bring out one or two for her to have a look at, so she pointed at a pipe that was just about the most ordinary-looking, with nothing excessive or flamboyant going on, and the shopkeeper pulled back the drawer, took it out and placed it gently on the glass, and Yuki could easily have spent another five minutes peering at it if he hadn't picked it up again and placed it in her hand.

The bowl seemed to sit quite happily in that soft pad of flesh between her thumb and forefinger. She tried latching her thumb over the stem where it joined the bowl, but this didn't feel at all right. And at this point the shopkeeper slipped his hand into his jacket pocket and brought out his own personal pipe. His grip was pretty similar to Yuki's, but instead of locking his thumb over the stem, he brought it up alongside the bowl. Then his other hand went into the opposite pocket and drew out a rectangular leather pouch – soft and worn and looking about a hundred years old. Still holding it in one hand, the shopkeeper adjusted his fingers and let the pouch fall open. Then dipped his pipe into the pouch, where it rummaged about for a moment until it re-emerged with his thumb over the top of the bowl and a few straggles of tobacco sprouting from under it. With the end of his thumb he cajoled the wayward strands into the bowl and tamped them down. The tobacco pouch was flipped shut and posted back in his pocket. Then he nudged a wooden caddy of tobacco across the counter towards Yukiko.

It was harder than it looked. Yuki was determined to only use one hand, but overfilled the bowl, so that no amount of tamping would pack it all in. All the same, the shopkeeper didn't wince or mock her. He just kept on quietly watching, making occasional encouraging noises until she'd worked out what was more or less the right amount.

She emptied the tobacco back into the wooden caddy and tried some other pipes, but kept returning to that first one. She liked the fact that it was small and neat, with a cherry-red bowl, all super-shiny. And the more she held it the more she liked it until finally she went ahead and bought the thing.

She's taken it out now and again, but never in front of Kumiko – when she's been on her own, in the hope that having it nipped between her teeth would help her concentrate, and once or twice as she stood before the mirror in Kumi's bedroom, to deliver some mimed oratory, using the stem as a little dagger, to add emphasis to particular words.

Sitting on a bench near Leicester Square she gripped it in her pocket and dared herself to take it out. She finally managed to do so only when a middle-aged woman came along, dragging two small children in her wake. She was making such a big deal about how tough it was looking after these children and broadcasting every instruction to the rest of the world. So as they approached, Yuki pulled out the pipe and popped it in her mouth. As the kids went by they had a good, long look at her, and Yuki gave them a big old wink in return. Like some pipe-smoking character from a British movie from the Fifties. Or how she imagined that big, bald guy might wink at someone, when he was relaxing after a little midday sex with his mistress, as happy as a bear.

When Yuki finally gets to her feet about half an hour later her ass is so cold she can barely feel it. I'm going to have to have it surgically removed, she thinks. Then she slowly climbs the stile and heads down the moors towards Haworth.

Having spent so much time in the company of the Crazy Elders and, prior to that, Kumiko and her friends, she now finds it odd not to be part of some larger company. So as she strides along she thinks to herself, Here is Yukiko, making her way through the English landscape. Yukiko, finally on her own.

Despite her plan to try and avoid the village's more popular areas she's now so worn down with the cold that she heads into the first teashop, just to restore a little heat. She manages to order a coffee, tucks herself away in a corner and for the best part of an hour reads a magazine, taking tiny sips from her cup.

When she's done she heads back up the high street, manages to find the lane along which they all came trotting into town this morning and walks back down it, to the car park. She slows right down as she reaches the corner – tiptoes up to it and carefully peeps around – to find that the coach really has left without her. But instead of feeling thrilled and liberated, as she expected, she finds she's a little put out. Imagine that, she thinks. Going off without me. Leaving a poor little Japanese girl all on her own.

*

Yuki really was convinced she'd be able to find the hotel unaided. The town's not so very big, after all. Plus, some sixth sense would surely draw her towards it. And yet she walks up and down any number of streets without encountering the door she's after. Perhaps they've changed it? Just to spite her. To stop her getting at the truth.

A couple of times she attempts to retrace her steps and becomes disoriented. There are people she knows who think getting lost is somehow exciting. A short cut to adventures. But to Yuki it is like an illness of the soul. You begin to disappear. Then there's the *looking* lost, which is almost as dreadful. All that halting, faltering progress. The pathetic air of bewilderment, with the stench of panic seeping from your skin.

In the end, she gives up and heads for the Tourist Information Centre – the over-lit little office she first noticed this morning on the way into town. She manages to creep in while the woman behind the counter is turned away, talking to someone in the back room. And, man, this woman can really talk. What chance has little Yuki of understanding someone who delivers English at such speed, and with such commitment? So she scans all the racks and noticeboards for any sign of the Grosvenor Hotel. There's information regarding places to eat, places to walk, places from which to take a steam train, as well as very many places to lay one's head at the close of day, but no obvious information relating to the particular hotel Yuki is after – none, at least, in pictorial form.

Finally, Yuki picks up an OS map of the area which she'll probably require in her investigation, takes a deep breath and approaches the counter, gently waving it in the air. Greets the Information Lady just as she's been taught, with a bright Hello. Places the map on the counter. Hands the woman a ten-pound note and, as she's taking the change, and without any thought towards constructing a meaningful question in which to give it context, jumps right on in and attempts to pronounce the name of the hotel. Just kind of coughs it up like a hairball and spits it out into the room.

The Information Lady looks back at Yuki, apparently baffled, and at Yuki's second attempt studies her mouth, to see if she might recognise the words as they're being formed.

All this attention is doing nothing but make Yuki more uncomfortable. She tries again, a little louder, and with extra emphasis on the first syllable. Then finally raises a hand. Bends down and pulls out of her rucksack the folded envelope, with its frayed old corners. Takes out the photographs and, like a poker player, fans them out in her hands. She picks out the one she's after and places it down on the counter. The Information Lady moves a finger towards it. Oh, please don't touch it, thinks Yuki. It's bad enough I'm letting you even look at the thing.

In the photograph, Yukiko's mother stands on the steps before what seems to Yukiko to be a very English front door. On her mother's face is that same expression. Her eyes shine, but a smile has yet to materialise. One day, Yukiko is convinced, she will pick up this or any other photograph and the smile will have finally arrived.

Oh, the *Grosvenor*, says the Information Lady.

And Yukiko thinks, Now, how the hell would I ever have imagined that those letters, in that order, would sound that way?

The Information Lady offers to call the hotel to check that a room is available, miming the picking up of a telephone receiver, but Yuki declines. Let's keep any chitter-chat to an absolute minimum, shall we? she thinks. So the Information Lady plucks up a Haworth street map, spins it round on the counter so that it faces Yuki and draws an asterisk to mark their current location, another where Yuki is headed and a little line that winds along the streets between the two.

*

Yukiko reaches the hotel in less than five minutes and is initially flummoxed. The word *Hotel* suggests an establishment of some stature – big enough, at least, to maintain one's anonymity. But this is essentially just a large English house with the words 'Grosvenor Hotel' stencilled in a retro font onto the glass above the door. All the same, it is without doubt the same doorway her mother posed before in the photograph and for that she is tremendously grateful. She climbs the steps and whacks the knocker against the door a couple of times.

The woman who opens the door is in her sixties maybe, but not quite as old as Mrs Kudo and company. Once she's hauled back the door she gives Yuki a big smile, which is much appreciated. And it occurs to Yuki that she should have maybe rehearsed a handful of words regarding the requesting of a room. Instead, she lifts the OS map and the street map. As if to say, I'm a Foreign Tourist Person. Do you really want to hear me desecrate your language? And this seems to suffice, because the woman steps back, to allow Yuki to come on in.

The hall is a little overwhelming. There's an old table covered with stacks of leaflets. The walls are filled with framed prints and old photographs. The carpet is its own geometric universe of greens and oranges, which by one doorway intersects with something predominantly pink and floral. Yuki makes a mental note to come back later and take a photograph or two.

The woman holds out a laminated list with the cost of a room printed on it – a figure which to Yuki seems wholly acceptable. Then, once she's written her name in an upholstered ledger, the woman leads Yuki across the hall into the dining room.

As they stand on the threshold, the woman explains

that they no longer offer evening meals. We're really just a B & B, she says. And, seeing Yukiko's look of bewilderment, she does her best to explain what a 'B & B' is.

She slips through another door, re-emerges with a key in her hand, then leads Yuki on up the stairs. The bedroom has a big old bed in it and lots of large, brown furniture. Yuki looks around for a door to an en-suite bathroom. Where's a person meant to do their pee-pee? she wonders. In the sink?

The B & B Lady beckons Yuki to follow and opens a door across the corridor. Steps back, to let Yuki pop her head in there – a tiny room with a massive bath, and a toilet and sink right beside. The woman smiles and Yuki smiles right back, nodding madly. Perfect! Now I can brush my teeth whilst sitting on the lavatory.

As soon as she has the key and the B & B Lady has left her to it, Yuki climbs up onto the enormous bed. Thinks, I could fall asleep – right now, in these cold, damp clothes. I might not wake for a month or more. The sun would slowly swing by the window. People would go up and down the street, oblivious. And when I finally woke, all my little obsessions would've been smoothed away and my life would be solved, like a puzzle. I'd have a cup of tea at one of the little tables in the dining room, pay the bill, take the elevator down to Haworth International and fly straight home.

Eventually, she sits herself up, takes out the folded envelope and picks through the photographs. Finds the one of an open window and carries it over to the window in her room. She pulls the net curtain back and stares across the street. Not bad, she thinks. In the photograph, a dressing table stands in the foreground, with paper and pens spread across it. The window's open, and clearly visible in the distance is the house across the street. It's the same house that Yukiko can now see, but from a slightly different angle. A little to the left of where it should be. But to have come all this way and to be this close, thinks Yuki. That really is not so bad at all.

Yuki takes off her damp clothes, hangs them over radiators and the backs of chairs and wraps herself up in a large white towel. She sits on the edge of the bed and calls her sister, but there's no answer, so she leaves a message. There's been a bit of a mix-up, she says. Give me a call. Then hangs up, double-quick. Thinks, Well, that should put a little heat under her.

She unpacks and has a little tour of the room, checking out all the furniture and fittings. Everything really is quite old. She goes over to the door, quietly opens it and looks up and down the corridor. Creeps over to the bathroom. Has another glance at the massive bath and ancient lavatory. Then goes tiptoeing down the corridor, to the next door along.

All the time she tells herself, If someone suddenly appears I'll just pretend I was looking for the bathroom. I'm Japanese. I haven't a clue.

She stops by the door – and listens. Has another look back down the corridor. Then leans forward and puts her eye right up to the keyhole.

She can see the bed, and a set of drawers beyond it, but not much more. Maybe the window is further round to the right. And yet there's something about the light. The quality of the light in there feels much warmer. Is that possible? That the light in one room can be that much warmer than the one next door?

She gets to her feet and wraps her palm around the handle. So sorry, she says to herself. I thought this was the bathroom. Turns the handle . . . so, so slowly . . . all the way . . . and pushes. Is almost relieved to find the door is locked. Then half-convinces herself there really is some noise, off down the stairs. Someone coming. And scurries back to the safety of her own room.

She climbs under the duvet, to warm herself up, but within a minute she's thinking, This isn't working. My temperature's dropped below some critical point. So she kicks back the sheets, picks out some dry clothes and heads to the bathroom.

She sits on the lavatory seat, watching the water come chug, chug, chugging into the worn enamel. I should take some pics, she thinks. Of the linoleum, all creased and cracked in the corner. The pipes under the sink, rusty at the junctions. The timber rotting beneath the paint in the window frame.

She checks the lock before undoing her towel, jams her trainers under the door for extra security and steps into the bath. The water must be half a metre deep. She thinks, Perhaps the English don't actually use so much water? But if not, why have such super-deep baths?

She sits with the water up around her ribs for a moment. Then takes a breath, lies back and lets all that hot, hot water come rolling over her shoulders. And she is gone.

The last few years when Yuki lies back in the bath she always thinks of her mother. Her aching-deep, motherly love. Maybe it goes right back to her mother bathing her, when she was a baby. Maybe it's the same with everyone. When she was nine or ten Yuki would let the weight of her body drag her right down until she was flat out and her head went under, and she could feel her hair gently floating all around. Then she would count – to thirty . . . forty . . . fifty. To see how long she could stay down there. The trick, she worked out, is to try and relax – especially around the shoulders. To try and keep at bay the quite reasonable fear that you've just taken your very last breath. You tell yourself, Just try and stick it out for another few seconds. And you let a few bubbles of air out through your mouth. Then again, Just another second or two. Until it really is too, too much, you feel you're about to burst or pass out and know that you absolutely must get some air back inside you, before the blackness moves on in. And you come up in a great burst of water. Panting, frantic. But, at the same time, exhilarated and feeling very good indeed.

Yukiko still occasionally does a little bathtime breath-holding. Enjoys that underwater feeling – of being both distant and ever so close. She's a great admirer of the Japanese freedivers Ryuzo Shinomiya and Shun Oshima.

Men who can fill their mighty lungs and go down, down, down like an eel, for a hundred and fifty metres. No earplugs. No wetsuits. Just mortal flesh in the ever-tightening grip of all that water pressure. Yukiko has often wondered what it must be like to feel the water go cold and black around you, as you push down, down, down . . . then down, down, down again.

She has some cuttings at home in one of her books. Two or three of Shinomiya and one of Loïc Leferme. She was flicking through the book a couple of days before she came out here when she noticed how, on the opposite page to the photograph of Leferme holding the rope, with all the black of the deep down below him, there was a photo from a magazine taken from some spacecraft, at the very edge of the earth's atmosphere. Half the picture is the pale blue earth, with a fine misty strip above it. The rest is just the deep, deep black of space. And it struck her how, despite having cut the pictures out of magazines weeks apart, they both represent the parameters of our existence – where there's nothing beyond but that abysmal blackness, dead and heavy.

Today she doesn't allow her face to go right under. Has reservations about doing so in an unfamiliar bath, in a foreign land. Clunking her head or getting her toe tangled in the plug chain and drowning here in North England would cause her profound psychic upset. Much more so than drowning in a bath back home.

So Yukiko slides on down as far as she can without her face actually going under water. Her toes barely touch the far end of the bath. She's pretty much floating, with the heat beginning to get right into her bones now, when she thinks she hears something. Lies there, listening, for a second – super-alert. First the suspicion, then the conviction that the sound she's hearing is her phone, back in the bedroom. Then all at once she's dragging herself up and climbing out of the bath, bringing all that water with her. Grabbing her towel, wrapping it round her and heading for the door. Her fingers slip on the lock. She has to crouch down and yank her trainers from under the door. Before going hurtling out into the hallway.

Then – whump!

She hits the floor before she knows what's happened – that her wet feet have shot out from under her on the bare floorboards. She's on her side with all the wind knocked right out of her. Her shoulder's hurting and she really is pretty shaken up. But once she's sure she hasn't broken anything she gets back to her feet, opens the door to her bedroom. Then limps over to the bed, grabs her phone and brings it up to her ear.

She swears into it. I fell, she says. Damn near broke my neck.

Yuki brings her shoulder round and studies it, to see if there's any major damage. Shit, she says, that really, really hurts.

Kumiko wants to know what the fuck is going on and why Yuki keeps calling her on her mobile when she knows she's at work and can't answer it. Also, what does she mean about there being a mix-up?

Yuki gives herself a moment, to try and conjure up the necessary indignation. She rubs her shoulder. Limps back over to the door and pushes it to. The damned coach, she says. The damned coach went off without her and left her stranded. She rolls herself onto the bed. I was there, where I was meant to meet them, but the damned coach must have set off early. Oh, she was so, so angry, she says.

There's a pause down the line from Kumiko. So where the fuck are you now?

Yuki explains how she's still in Haworth, but how, in a way, that's not such a bad thing. Because they'd only had a couple of hours to look around the village. Which is nothing like long enough. These tours are always in such a hurry to get on to the next place. So at least now she'll be able to have a proper look around.

Yukiko pauses, to see if Kumiko's got anything to say yet.

And where are you staying, she says.

Yuki tells her how she found this lovely little guest house. You should see the bath, she says. I was practically swimming from one end of it to the other when you called.

Another silence from Kumiko. Yuki does her damnedest not to jump on in and fill it up with bluster. She's making more of an effort these days in that respect.

Says, I'll probably just have another look around in the morning and get a train back in the afternoon.

What's it called?

What's what called?

Yukiko's looking round the room now. Can't think of anything.

The hotel. What's the name of the place where you've got a room?

It's the first English word that comes into Yuki's mind. The Brontë Hotel, she says. Then pulls a face to herself. It's a little bit scary. Just full of loads of weird old Brontë stuff.

Kumiko seems to be calming down a little. She says she just wants to be sure Yuki hasn't gone mad or anything. That you're not going to go wandering off onto the moors and disappear.

No way, she says. I'm just going to have a look around the village.

Another little Kumiko silence. Then she says, I know what you're doing, Yuki. You're so goddamned morbid.

Yuki is tempted to plead ignorance, or pretend to be offended. But that would only encourage Kumiko to lecture her some more. It's actually quite a sweet little place, she says. And looks around the room. Then – she doesn't know why, she just can't seem to help herself – she says, I've decided when I get home I'm going to read all the Brontë novels, one after the other. Possibly in English.

She can hear Kumiko sighing. Or maybe laughing, in an exasperated sort of way.

You're like a child, she says. Like a goddamned child.

The day after she arrived in London Yuki took the tube into town with Kumiko and was down at the railings of Buckingham Palace before eight, with the roads all packed with traffic but not another tourist yet in sight. She'd told Kumiko she planned to go to Covent Garden to get some breakfast, then on to a gallery or two. If she'd told her her real intentions Kumiko would've probably laughed in her face.

She'd come across the photograph pretty much by accident. She was searching through a whole bunch of images of girls screaming in the 1960s, so was more or less guaranteed to end up with some shots of Beatles fans. She's looked at the picture so many times since she can bring to mind a dozen details without any effort – how one particular girl's hair falls across her face, the design on another girl's knee socks, etc. – but, curiously, has trouble seeing the picture as a whole. Just lots of tiny details, all mixed up in her head.

There are, in fact, two different versions of the photograph, one more tightly cropped than the other, with fewer policemen in the shot. It adds a little more intensity, as if you're right in the middle of all this craziness, whereas Yuki actually prefers the wider shot and the consequent perspective. The overall shape of the thing.

The girls – and the crowd consists almost entirely of teenage girls – are going wild about The Beatles. Since most of the screaming girls and the policemen who're doing their best to contain them have their faces turned to the left of the frame Yuki assumes that The Beatles have either just driven by and are heading on into the palace, or finished doing whatever they're doing in the palace and are about to come back out. In the foreground, five policemen are standing, arms linked and legs apart getting pushed and pulled in ten different directions, with all that teenage female emotion raging away at their backs. One policeman's helmet is tipped over his eyes, as if it's about to go flying. The policeman to his right leans back, mouth open, apparently gasping for air.

Then there are the girls – sobbing, screaming, arms flailing. The two most clearly visible, on either side of the policeman whose helmet is about to hit the ground, are caught in pleasing symmetry, right foot back, pushing off the ground, left foot forward and up on the toes. Their skirts stop just above the knee. So not yet quite a mini. The girl on the left is blonde and seems to be shouting, eyes wide open. The girl on the right is dark-haired and could almost be laughing, eyes squeezed tight shut. Their arms are all tangled up with those of the policemen. There's no apparent ill-will from either contingent, and yet the sense of suspended energy almost knocks you off your feet.

When Yuki reached the palace's railings she saw how there were, in fact, three different gates to choose from, but by bringing the photo up on her phone and studying the various columns and wrought-iron ornaments in the background managed to work out where the girls had been. She strolled on over with the photograph still up on her phone and adjusted her position until the proportions of the columns were more or less equal and the railings stretched off in a similar way. Then she brought the phone down and stared into the space where the policemen had leaned and struggled, and the girls had struggled and screamed. Again, she wondered what had become of those girls and policemen. What their memories of that particular moment were. And, again, considered the practicalities involved in trying to trace them. In bringing them back here to have them assume the exact same pose.

The first time she saw the photograph she didn't notice the professional stills camera held aloft in the middle of the girls, as if its owner was trying to keep it dry whilst crossing a river. Or the movie camera, just inside the frame over to the right. And it was only on a later viewing that she finally noticed the guy at the back, leaning in, with an old-fashioned pair of headphones clamped to his head, like some sort of spy from the ordinary world. So, not only were these moments being caught by several stills photographers and at least one movie camera, but someone was recording the actual *sound*. Because in this instance, Yuki feels, the sound is the crucial element. The medium where the event's real power resides. Imagine bringing each participant back and having them take up their position. Telling them to close their eyes and remember that day, fifty years ago. Maybe expose them to some sort of collective hypnosis, or just have them meditate upon the photograph. To have them reach right down and try and recover their younger selves, their teenage preoccupations. Then very slowly, on gigantic speakers, you'd bring up the original recorded sound. What would happen inside those people? What would happen to the fabric of our world?

Yukiko has seen plenty of movie footage of Beatles fans from the same sort of period. Highly strung young girls perched in their seats with the band performing off in the distance. You can see the girls winding themselves up – simultaneously a part of the overall frenzy yet disappearing into their own very personal teenage trance. They bring their fists up to their mouths . . . take a breath, of something overpowering . . . then start to scream and shake their head. It looks so pure. So beautifully pure and intense.

When she wakes almost an hour and a half later the world has grown cold and dark around her. And having slept while the last trace of daylight drained away unsettles her, as if she's woken beneath a stone.

She pulls on her dressing gown, retrieves her things from the bathroom and mops up the water on the floor in the corridor where she fell. For a minute or two she sits on the edge of the bed, still tired and fuggy. Then she takes out her mother's blue blouse and silk headscarf, stands before the mirror and puts them on.

In the photograph taken outside the parsonage her mother wears the same scarf knotted round her neck. The cream coat is long gone, but the blouse is from the same period, and when she has it on and can feel it soft and sleek against her Yuki imagines the warmth of her flesh somehow reinvigorating the material – putting it in mind of being warmed by her mother's skin.

She washes her face and cleans her teeth at the sink. Pictures her mother doing these same small things next door, with just a wall between them – the two of them leaning in towards each other.

Some people, possibly out of a misguided sense of

kindness, have said that Yuki looks like her mother, but she can't see it. What they share, she thinks, is the same fretful nature. The tendency to keep on picking away at something long past the point when it's likely to do any good.

She has one last look in the mirror – at her standing in her mother's clothes. Then grabs her coat, goes down the stairs, across the geometric carpet and out into the cold, old town.

The streets are pretty much empty. The people who went up and down the pavements a few hours earlier are now back home, slumped in front of their TVs. Or, like Mrs Kudo and the other Elders, gathered in a hotel bar, talking, drinking and pecking at bowls of nuts.

Within a few minutes she reaches the little lane that leads to the parsonage and heads on up it, past the ancient graveyard with its monstrous trees. A tall wooden gate blocks the steps Yuki took this morning. So there's nothing to see of the parsonage but the vast blank wall at its side. Yuki stands and stares up at it, quite impassive. Plenty of other people must've tried to break in, she thinks. Brontë Obsessives. The Brontë Deranged. But they'd almost certainly have tried to gain entry via the doors and windows. Whereas Yukiko now sees that the way to do it would be to shimmy up the drainpipe, climb onto the roof, pull up four or five of those old tiles and squeeze down into the loft. Then it would just be a matter of kicking a decent-sized hole through the ceiling and dropping onto the landing. In no time at all you'd be buttoning yourself into Charlotte's pale paisley dress, to go exploring the place at your leisure – poking your head into all the interesting little corners you're not normally allowed anywhere near.

Of course, the staff wouldn't appreciate you barricading yourself into their precious parsonage. Wouldn't be at all pleased to turn up for work and find the front door wedged shut with Emily's Death Bed. They'd call the cops. Shout down the phone at them, about how some crazy Jap had broken in and was wandering around in Charlotte's dress and Emily's No. 1 bonnet. But, other than a great deal of complaining, really, what could they do?

Curiously, now that she's standing here, right beside the parsonage, the one thing she'd really like to get her hands on is that little lock of Charlotte's hair. How incredibly strange, she thinks, to trim a lock of hair from a young dead woman. Did they imagine it might carry some of Charlotte's spirit? Some clue to her literary talent? And yet here Yuki is, in her dead mother's clothes, a couple of hundred years later, and not at all the conventional Brontë Fan, but desperately wanting to feel between her fingers the hair that once grew on poor Charlotte's head.

Yuki has a good look at the gate. It's quite conceivable, she thinks, that with a little scuffling and scrambling, she might manage to clamber over it. There are tiny gaps and recesses in the stone posts on both sides where her feet might go. But she's already got a smashed-up shoulder and another fall would almost certainly kill her. She doubts she'd be able to accommodate the pain. So she begins to wonder if there's maybe a way of climbing the wall back down the lane, over into the graveyard, to get to the wall at the bottom of the parsonage garden, which may not be as tall as the one bearing down on her here.

It's worth a go, she thinks, so strolls back down the alley, looking for a section of wall she might have a hope of getting over. The top of the wall comes up to her shoulder, so Yuki sees how she's going to have to compensate for her lack of natural ability in the climbing department with maximum explosive energy. She glances up and down the lane to check that no one's coming, takes a breath, then just sort of hurls herself at it. She throws her good arm up and over. Her hand takes a hold of wet moss, with cold stone beneath. Well, it's too late now, she thinks, to be bothering about such unpleasantness. From here on in it may very well be nothing but wet moss and cold, cold stone.

Her feet keep on scrambling until she manages to get one knee over the top. Then the rest of her, so she's just kind of lying there hugging the wall, with a leg and arm hanging down on either side. She takes a breath, slowly swings her ass over and lowers herself into what feels like a very dark pit.

When both feet finally reach the ground she turns and stands in the solid darkness. Maybe this wasn't such a neat idea, she thinks.

She's waiting for her eyes to adjust – to begin to pick

out any sort of form or features. Then she has an idea. Pulls out her phone, taps the screen and its dim blue light almost lifts the graves from the gloom. She plots a vague course, braces herself and sets off between the gravestones. You see, Mother, she says to herself. You see what I am prepared to do for you?

Yuki has no way of knowing where each foot is falling. Whether it will find something firm or just keep falling, through the leaves and soft, wet earth. She edges round the first headstone and is heading on to the next one when the light on her phone cuts out and she's dropped back into darkness. She stops. Fumbles for another button. Tells herself, Just don't drop the goddamned phone. And when the blue light returns and she has steadied herself, she goes on again, on towards the next grave, with the phone held up in one hand and the other sweeping left and right before her, trying to fend off anything that might be in her way.

She creeps between the gravestones, tapping at the screen of her phone at regular intervals until another wall slowly takes shape in the distance – a wall that is thankfully nowhere near as tall as the one by the gate. She hauls herself up onto it, swings both legs over and drops down into the garden on the other side.

She stands and waits – for blinding floodlights to clank into action. For some mind-jangling alarm to be triggered and tear the night apart. But it's still just Yuki in the dark and the silence. And now that she's clear of the graveyard's trees she has a little more sky above her and her surroundings are a little better known to her. There must be creatures, she thinks, tiny night-time creatures. Yuki imagines them, standing frozen in the darkness – wondering who the hell this is, crashing through their private habitat. For a moment she stands among them, listening. Then creeps across the lawns and gardens and on up to the house.

The parsonage looks even grimmer in the dark than it does by daylight. Like a colossal Brontë gravestone, set back from all the rest. It stands so grand and arrogant that Yuki is sorely tempted to inflict upon it some minor act of desecration. To chip away at one of its walls, say. Or scrape off a little sliver of paintwork. If she had the courage she'd find a rock and throw it at one of the windows. She likes to imagine that she would. But the house has such an almighty malevolent presence Yuki is sure if she went within a metre of it she'd be dragged in, swallowed up and never heard of again.

She tiptoes up onto the flagstones. Keeps glancing back over at the churchyard – to try and get her bearings and be sure of her means of escape. She finds the spot where she crouched this morning and clung to her inhaler. Then the place where her mother stood and posed for the photograph. And she takes up her position again, with her back to the parsonage. Is quite sure that some trace of her mother must be maintained here somewhere – in the old stone beneath her feet, or some remnant of breath, caught in a web beneath a window sill. And though she can sense the presence of her mother, it really is no more than what she senses any other day. So she unknots the headscarf, opens it out and folds it along the diagonal. Lifts it over her head and ties it under her chin. And even as she does so she feels something shift and give inside her, like a small door opening onto a distant, busy place. It may just be the feel of the silk between her fingers, or that the act of folding the scarf has broken open some scent locked in its fine, tight weave. But as Yuki stands there in her mother's scarf and blouse, recreating that earlier photograph when her mother was here in the North of England and apparently happy, before heading back home where she seemed to quickly go quite mad, Yuki has a sudden, overwhelming sense of her mother being right there with her.

Then the terrible longing rises up in her. Fills her up in an instant, until there's nothing but the longing. And the pain and weight of it is too, too much. But even as she's trying to comprehend what she feels – what moves and turns inside her – her mother and her love begin to slip away.

No, she says – almost audible. But the more she reaches for her, tries to retrieve her, the quicker she seems to slip away.

Until she's gone. Back to her typical proximity, within hearing but just out of sight. And Yuki crouches – all pain and heartbreak – facing the very spot where she'd sat and struggled to catch her breath earlier in the day.

It takes a while for her to return to herself. To be reinstated. She gets to her feet and stares at the cold, dark garden. Then turns and looks back up at the house. Thinks, If every person who came here took just one small scrap of the wretched house away with them, in no time at all there'd be nothing left but a whole bunch of dust and rubble. And maybe the world would be a better place.

She takes a step or two towards the parsonage, perfectly aware of the consequences. Goes right up to it, feeling for a coin in her pocket. And having found one, brings it out, leans in and starts to dig away at the stone. A couple of crumbs fall into her hand and she closes her fist around them. This is coming home with me, she tells the house. All the way back to goddamned Japan. And you will never ever see it again, you miserable goddamned fucker.

She drops the bits of stone and the coin back into her pocket, turns and sets off across the garden. Knows very well what's going to happen. Can already feel the rage of the place funnel up and begin to roll out into the darkness. Feels it come tumbling after her as she hobbles across the lawn. Thinks, Maybe this is what I want.

She reaches the wall, but finds it almost impossible to climb back up it. The ground must somehow be lower on this side. But she scrambles away, feeling that terrible malevolence moving in on her. And is beginning to regret her actions now, just as she knew she would – her feet skittering away at the wall and her going nowhere. Then finally, finally gaining traction, scrambling up, over and into the graveyard. But with that weight of evil almost upon her and not having the time to bring out her phone. So going clattering between the gravestones in complete darkness. Catching her shin on one, her hip on another, as if she's running a gauntlet of stone. And not at all sure which way she's heading, or whether she'll ever find her way out of here. Finally running into a wall so hard that it smacks her in the chest and knocks the wind right out of her. Not having a clue what wall it is, what's on the other side. But clambering up, flipping herself around, then letting herself fall.

She lands in a heap on the cobbles. But, far from feeling released, it's as if she's brought half the graveyard over the wall with her, like some dreadful sediment. She gets to her feet and all the bumps and scratches seem to suddenly come alive to her – across her hands and arms, down both her legs. I may have to ask the B & B Lady for some sort of English ointment, she thinks. May have to convert my room into a place of convalescence.

She brushes herself down then turns, with the intention of heading back towards the high street, and has barely limped any sort of distance when she has the powerful sense of someone else being there in the alley with her. She turns around and sees a figure standing, watching, not far away.

Yuki is so thoroughly taken aback that she sort of yelps, quite involuntarily. The girl doesn't move. Just carries on watching. And Yuki's next thought is that this girl, whoever she is, must've been there when she came lumbering over the wall just now. May have even seen her go creeping into the graveyard ten minutes earlier. All of this rushes through her mind as the girl continues to stare at her. Then Yuki turns and heads away, back down the alley. She keeps on walking – hurrying now – but can't stop herself from having one last look over her shoulder. Just a teenage girl with blonde hair, hands tucked into her coat pockets – standing and watching, silent.

Yuki reaches the high street and limps on down it, quite distracted. It's the sort of thing, she knows, that will get right under her skin if she's not careful. Because what was meant to be a private act – her own peculiar little ritual – now appears to have been compromised. As if a strange young girl having witnessed Yuki creeping away from the parsonage has cut a nick in her entire Psychic Brontë Enterprise and threatened to let all the superstition and voodoo escape.

Yukiko's scuttling down the road, back towards the B & B, with all the cuts and bruises raging about her, when she passes a pub, catches a blast of hot food and realises that the last time she ate was at the little picnic out on the moors. So she carries on down the high street, to the one shop still throwing light out onto the pavement. She picks out some cellophane-encased savoury pastry from a cooler, a two-litre bottle of Coke from the fridge and, after some deliberation, commits to a souvenir tin of Brontë biscuits, with all three sisters staring glumly from the lid.

If she doesn't buy it now, she knows, she'll only come

back and buy it tomorrow. Her only dilemma is whether to give it to Kumiko or keep it for herself. She's doing her best to pay the woman behind the counter by offering her various bank notes . . . How much do you need? Just *take* it! Take it all! . . . when she remembers she still has her mother's headscarf up over her hair. If I was wearing my Jackie O sunglasses, she thinks, it might make a little more sense.

She limps back up the hill. Her left hip, her right shoulder and the knuckles of her right hand are all pretty painful – but she's feeling a little calmer. Perhaps because she has some food, and is already picturing herself lying in bed, watching TV, eating. With a couple of drinks working away inside of her.

She reaches her street and is counting down the doors to the B & B – can already see it up ahead – when she again has that sense of someone close by, watching. She waits until she's right at the door, with the key in the lock, before allowing herself to turn around. And there, no more than twenty metres away, on the other side of the street, is the same girl who was standing in the lane beside the parsonage. Yukiko looks straight at her but, again, the girl doesn't seem the least bit embarrassed and keeps on staring right back at her.

The evening slides by very nicely, thank you. Yukiko takes the bottle of Jameson from her rucksack, pours a couple of belts of it into the glass from the bedside table and tops it up with Coke. Turns on the TV and opens up the cheese and onion pastry. Then, to keep the Coke good and cold, she opens the window and tucks it away, right in the corner of the ledge. There's barely a breeze out there, so it seems pretty unlikely it's going to fall and take out someone heading down the pavement. She looks across the street, half expecting to see the ghost of a girl still standing on the pavement and gawping up at her, but she's gone.

Her first drink lasts barely five minutes. And by the time Yuki's filled her glass for a second, then a third time she realises her shoulder has suddenly stopped aching. She can feel some crunching as she shifts it in its socket, as if a little grit has got in there somehow. But there's no great pain or discomfort. She lifts the glass up to the light and thinks, Man, this stuff is good.

She undresses. Her mother's blouse is plucked and scratched from all the clambering over walls and clattering between gravestones, but Yuki finds this doesn't particularly bother her. She checks out all her little cuts and bruises. My poor, poor body, she thinks. Then climbs under the covers and flicks through the channels, looking for a horror film with practically no dialogue, or something so uncompromisingly English that it'll be like watching a film from outer space.

She tops up her glass another time or two. Then is suddenly gripped by an all-encompassing hunger. The pastry's long gone but Yuki remembers the biscuits. Souvenir Brontë Biscuits are exactly what she needs right now. But the Brontë Biscuit Tin is reluctant to surrender its contents to some drunk young woman. A strip of sticky tape has the lid pretty much welded to the tin. It must take Yukiko the best part of five minutes just to locate the end of it and another couple to pluck enough of it up with her fingernail to be able to pinch it between her finger and thumb. Then, as she peels it back, the tape keeps splitting, but Yuki is determined that it will come off whole, rather than in lots of little strips. Damn you, Brontë Biscuit Tin!

When she finally manages to remove the lid Yuki is deeply disappointed. She'd hoped the biscuits might be Charlotte- and Emily-shaped. Or that, at the very least, there might be moulded representations of their faces in the chocolate. But there's nothing remotely Brontë-related going on here. Just eight or so separate silos, with a differently crimped or textured biscuit stacked in each one. Yukiko picks a couple out. Then makes her way methodically around the rest of them. Has a little breather while she pours herself another whiskey, then goes around again.

One of the TV channels is showing an American movie from the late 1980s, though Yuki doesn't recognise any of the actors. It looks like the kind of movie that is more or less guaranteed to feature someone jumping through a plate-glass window and falling, in slo-mo, from a very great height.

Yuki starts to think about the room next door, where her mother slept. Turns down the TV and creeps over to the adjoining wall. Puts her ear up to it and listens. Then she goes over to her door, out into the corridor and heads along it a little way. If anyone was in there, she thinks, there'd be some light coming under the door, or noise of some sort. But there's nothing. So she goes back to her room, climbs back into bed and stares at the wall a little more.

Another couple of Jameson and Cokes, she thinks, and she might well roll back the carpet, yank up a couple of floorboards and crawl right on through there. Sure, she'd get covered in dust and pick up even more cuts and bruises, but it'd be worth it just to have a look around. Then she remembers the tiny toys they discovered under the floor at the parsonage – little toy soldiers and wooden blocks that the infant sisters must have played with. And is so deeply moved, so filled with love and hurt that she just knows she must tell Kumi all about this, right away.

Kumiko's phone rings twice before it cuts to the message and Yuki's talking before she hears the beep.

Saying how she'd forgotten to mention earlier about these tiny books she saw at the parsonage. Sweet little things, all handwritten and stitched by the Brontës. Just like the two of them used to make when they were children, but even smaller, with little drawings of tiny sailing-ships and sitting rooms and someone standing by a tree. And writing so intricate, so absolutely microscopic you'd think a mouse had done it. Enough to break your heart.

As she speaks she notices she's having trouble with her pronunciation. Like driving a car with soft tyres that keeps on slipping on the bends. But she perseveres. She talks about the movie she's watching and how she's hoping for some big bust-up or car chase. Talks about the characters' incredible clothes and hair. Then suddenly runs out of steam. Stops. Yawns into the phone. Says Goodbye and hangs up.

She lies on her stomach, with her head at the base of the bed. Tells herself she'll give the movie another half hour or so. But within a few seconds she's beginning to nod off. So she turns the TV off, cleans her teeth and climbs back up onto her big old bed. Turns out the light, puts her head on the pillow and, just like Shinomiya and Oshima, drops down, down into the depths and darkness, as heavy as a stone.

*

For hour upon hour she rolls and turns in sleep. Weighed down by alcohol and half-oblivious to her dreams. Then, quite suddenly it seems, there is some sort of calamity. She is in danger, desperate. She sees the water's surface high above her, with nothing like enough breath to reach it, and comes racing back towards consciousness, practically throwing herself from the bed.

Almost immediately she comes up against a wall – solid and unforgiving, her mind still trapped down below, while in the flesh she slips and flounders. Her hands sweep across cold wallpaper. She thinks, I have to hold my nerve and work my way across it. Try to find some crack or schism. She is in a room, it would seem. Being kept prisoner, in the dark. Then her left hand takes hold of some material, thick and plentiful. And she pulls it back to find the streetlight. Then she remembers England. About being in Brontë Country. Looking for her mum.

And the world comes flooding back and she breathes, breathes – brimming with adrenaline. Stares down at the street, her heart pounding madly. The whiskey is burning in her stomach so she goes over to the sink and takes a drink straight from the tap. Stands there, still recovering. Thinks, this happens every month or two. I come hurtling up out of some dreadful torment and by the time I've worked out where I am, the dream's disintegrated – has folded back in on itself and slipped from view.

She has the light on now. Goes over to her rucksack and rummages among the few things still left in there till she finds the little headtorch she bought in London for just such night-fears. Turns the light out again, closes the curtains, and once her torch is switched on uses it to find her way back to bed. I'll keep it in my hand, she thinks. It'll help me stay calm until I get back off to sleep. But pretty soon she pulls it onto her head, with the elasticated straps holding it in place. Sits up against the pillow for a full five minutes, checking the messages on her phone. Then looks up, letting the light swing slowly from one corner of the ceiling to the other. Thinks, I should've had this with me when I was blundering round the graveyard.

Until at last she feels sleep begin to move back in on her. She looks over at the window with the curtain still open a little and thinks about the Coke out there in the cold. How her Aunt Kyoko used to tell her that after giving her hair a brush she should pluck the hair from the bristles and put it out on the window ledge, so that the birds can take it and use it to build their nests. And even now she can't decide whether this is just the kind of stuff grown-ups love to tell a child to fill their little heads with nonsense or whether there aren't in fact at this particular moment tiny birds taking hair from window ledges all around the planet. Grateful birds picking up girls' hair and using it to make their nests.

L ong before the death of her mother, when she would suddenly have very good reason to take an interest in it, Yuki was already carrying out her own little snow experiments – odd exercises in melting and freezing that she could easily dismiss as faintly ridiculous now that she's no longer eight or nine years old. But if she can't always remember the detail of the experiments she can recall her commitment. As you get older, she thinks, it's all too easy to forget the serious business of being a child.

Her bedroom window had its own broad ledge and, below it, a small flat roof above her father's study. One winter, when it seemed to snow every day for weeks on end, Yuki opened her window to find a modest drift of snow, with its flat white surface facing her, pristine. She studied it for a while, then began to systematically destroy it. The next day she brought up a candle and matches and melted some snow in an old tin, which she held with a rag at the rim. First on the ledge of her window, then, when the wind kept blowing out the candle, on the desk just inside her room.

The previous year she'd seen a TV movie in which a bearded man traipsed about some snowy wilderness teetering on the edge of extinction, which had scared the life out of her. She remembers him packing snow into a small pan and melting it over a fire, to make tea or drinking water. So it's likely that Yuki was, in her way, exploring ideas relating to survival and mortality. Lying in bed at night she would imagine herself huddled in a shelter made from leaves and branches. As the wind roared she'd pull the sheets around her and think, Stay awake, Yuki chan. If you fall asleep you may never wake up again, like that beardy man out in the snow.

In part, she supposes, her experiments were simply investigations into transformation. Because, having melted the snow over the candle's flame, she'd then tuck the tin back out in the corner of the flat roof to see what effect the night's freezing temperatures would have on whatever was inside. She exposed quite a number of things to the cold that winter: lemon juice . . . detergent . . . raw egg. She might even have logged her findings. In between, she would drip hot wax onto the back of her hand, as if she was being tortured. After that first shock of heat, when it seemed the wax would burn right through her, she'd see the wax quickly shift from clear oil to something milky. The pain would abate and the wax would stiffen, until she could pull it up, still warm but pliable and carrying a perfect imprint of every hair and pore on her skin.

Her little experiments continued right up to the point when the tin became so blackened it looked ready to shatter and she was having to reach further and further out onto the roof to retrieve some untouched snow. Sometimes Yuki thinks that, given the right encouragement, she could've been a chemist of some repute. She imagines herself standing, proud, in her lab coat, with a test tube pinched between her fingers. She looks quite serious – as befits a scientist of her rank.

It's still dark when Yuki's phone starts ringing. She has to drag herself out of what is, for once, a deeply restorative sleep. Sits herself up. Then has to try and find her phone, still ringing and lost among the sheets.

Before she's tracked it down she feels the pressure on her forehead, lifts a hand to it and finds the torch, still strapped in place. She locates the phone, sweeps the screen and brings it up to her ear. What, she says.

And without hesitation Kumiko is off, wanting to know precisely how much she drank last night. You sounded like some bum, she says. Like some degenerate. If you're not careful you're going to inflict some permanent physical damage.

Yuki climbs out of bed, arguing, quite reasonably, that Kumiko drinks far more than she does, but Kumi dismisses this. I'm bigger than you, she says. My liver's bigger. My liver could beat the shit out of that puny little liver of yours.

Yukiko's over at the mirror now, trying to disentangle the torch from her hair.

Also, Kumi says, why the hell were you getting so worked up about some little books the junior Brontës

89

made? Three days ago you knew practically nothing about these stupid women. Now you're talking like they're long-lost cousins. What is wrong with you?

Yukiko thinks, She called me this early on purpose. Knowing I'd still be sleeping and less likely to put up a decent fight. She leans in towards the mirror – there's a circular red mark in the skin where the torch was clamped against her forehead. I'm going to have to wear one of those awful beanies the rest of my life, she thinks. Or grow some ridiculous fringe.

What time it is, she says.

I don't know. About six thirty, says Kumiko. I've got an early meeting.

So why not call me after you've had the meeting? When you know I'll actually be awake?

I was *concerned*, she says. I turned my phone on just now and heard all your incoherent babble. And I thought, I need to check on my little sister straight away. Make sure she's not about to do anything *strange*.

This last comment, Yukiko knows, is just Kumiko fishing. She tells her to wait a second, puts her head under the tap and takes a couple of gulps of Yorkshire water. Wets her hand under the tap and wipes it across her face.

So when do you get back to town? Kumi wants to know.

Oh, I don't know. I need to look at the train times. Watching herself in the mirror, thinking, Look at that. Not even a flicker. I'm lying through my teeth and I didn't even blink.

Kumiko tells her to try and get back by five or six, so they can meet up after work. Taiki and Paul are talking about eating in Soho. And Yuki thinks, Well, that seals it. I'm just going to turn my phone off and stay up here for the rest of the week.

Kumiko says she has got to go. Makes Yuki promise she'll call when she's on her way, then hangs up.

Yuki limps off to the bathroom. Then tidies her room a little. She knows breakfast won't be served for another thirty minutes, so she takes out her mother's photos and the Ordnance Survey map and spends some time studying them. But pretty soon she's thinking, If I don't eat or drink something in the next ten minutes I may collapse, slip into a coma. So she pulls the bottle of Coke in off the window ledge and pops the lid off the tin of Brontë biscuits – just to get some sugar inside of her.

She washes and dresses super-slowly. Then finally decides she's had enough, picks up a couple of things and heads down the stairs. She wastes another few minutes looking at leaflets in the hallway, then goes on into the breakfast room. The table by the window is the only one with crockery and cutlery laid out on it, so she takes a seat at it.

She keeps herself busy by shifting her knife, fork and spoon about until they're all good and straight, but after a while thinks, Maybe I should make some sound, to let people know I'm actually sitting here. Or perhaps there's a little bell somewhere I'm supposed to ring?

Eventually she tells herself, This is crazy. So she gets up and creeps over to the kitchen door, which has those special hinges that allow the door to swing both ways. Yuki pushes gently at it, but instead of opening onto a busy kitchen with people dashing around, lots of steam and pots and pans, there's just an empty carpeted corridor.

She can hear a radio, off in the distance. Wonders whether she should call out, or maybe walk the extra couple of metres along to the corner. And as she's looking around she notices a row of hooks high up on the wall to her left with little bunches of keys hanging from them and pretty quickly works out what these keys are for. She's still standing there, staring at them, when the B & B Lady comes storming round the corner. Yukiko jumps, but the B & B Lady doesn't seem to mind her poking her head round the door. She's laughing and saying, Good morning, Good morning and a few other things Yuki can't quite make out as she leads her back to the table. Then, when Yuki's about to take her seat, the B & B Lady gives her a little pat on the shoulder. Really just the gentlest squeeze of affection, but to Yuki it feels like just about the best thing to have happened to her for quite a while.

Once she's settled in her chair the B & B Lady hands Yuki a menu and starts talking through the main four or five options, some of which have little sub-sections of their own. Yuki's thinking how much easier it would be if all the food was laid out in stainless-steel tubs, brightly lit, like they do in most hotels, so you can just pick out whatever food you happen to recognise. And in the end Yukiko just points at one of the options, says, Thank you. The B & B Lady nods and smiles and heads off back to the kitchen, and a few minutes later she's back with a pot of coffee and a couple of croissants, which is just fine as far as Yukiko's concerned, though it occurs to her that the way things are going she may eat nothing but bread, pastry and biscuits the whole time she's in this town.

When Yuki's finished and the B & B Lady comes out to take her plate, she leans back in her chair with some deliberation, so the B & B Lady can see the photos she's placed on the table. It's pretty clear, Yuki hopes, that she's trying to draw her attention to them because she's looking up at the B & B Lady, then back down at the photos, like a dog hoping you're going to pick up its ball. The B & B Lady moves on in for a closer look. One photo is just a tree or bush, bent right over by the wind. The other is a shot of one of the local reservoirs. Then Yukiko produces her Ordnance Survey map.

They have to clear everything off Yuki's table to make enough space to open the map out a little. The B & B Lady finds Haworth, looks back at the photos and checks that Yuki wants to know if she's any idea where the photos were taken.

Well, the tree, she says, and taps away at it. Where that tree is I've no idea. But the reservoir – I reckon I know where that is. And she lifts her finger, reaches over to the right a little, and places it on a patch of blue.

Yuki leans right in to study the spot beneath her finger. And, as the B & B Lady slowly withdraws it, brings her own finger in to make sure she doesn't let it slip away.

It takes Yuki a good hour or so to find her way out there. The directions are pretty clear, but towards the end of the journey she encounters a wall with barbed wire along the top and no obvious way round it, so she climbs up onto it to scan the moorland beyond, and it's only when she turns to jump back down that she sees the water glinting off in the distance, nowhere near where it's supposed to be.

She leaves the path and sets off through the heather towards it. The ground looks soft but is packed with stones and boulders, so Yuki has to watch every footfall and only sees the reservoir when she stops to make sure she's heading in the right direction. Then the ground begins to even out a little and she can smell the water in the air. She climbs a low stone wall. Takes out the photo and tries to work out where she should stand.

She goes on over to the right, but the photograph and the view before her seem determined not to correspond. Yuki wonders if she's maybe coming at the water from the wrong direction, but on the other side there's a much steeper bank, which wouldn't work at all. So she wanders up and down for another couple of minutes. Then finally just stands and looks out at the cold, grey water. Tiny waves shuffle back and forth at the water's edge, and way out in the middle the surface is being plucked up by the wind. Yuki thinks, Why would anyone want to take a photograph of this?

Before leaving Japan she pretty much assumed that she'd just step off the coach and things would start to fall into place straightaway. That her very presence here would get the wheels turning and that the curtain would slowly be lifted on everything. Sure, it felt good to stand outside the B & B and the parsonage and occupy the same space her mother had occupied ten years before. But there'd been no great revelation. Even creeping around in her mother's clothes hadn't been as productive as she'd expected. I must be a pretty poor psychic detective, she tells herself. If I was my captain I'd be considering taking my badge off me and kicking me out of the force.

As far as she knows, the Brontës didn't come out here to bathe or to do their laundry. It's not on any of the Brontë maps. The bent-back tree, at least, has some peculiar beauty to it. But even on a summer's day this water must look pretty dismal and not particularly mysterious.

When Yukiko's parents visited the UK her father stayed in London and her mum came up here on her own. Yuki has often been inclined to imagine that her mother may have had an affair of some sort. That there could have been a single, solitary man in her party. Or maybe even someone she arranged to meet up here. Well, perhaps this is where they came, to get away from all the others. To lie on the ground by the cold, grey water and fumble about under the North English sky.

She looks at the ground by her feet, as if she might yet find a trace of their bodies – some faint impression in the heather. She's got a carton of juice in her rucksack, but doesn't have the energy to wrestle it out of there. So she just squats down and has another look at the photograph – for some tiny detail she may have missed before.

She tries to line up the horizon in the photo with the one before her. Swings it slowly round from right to left to try and get it to bleed into the landscape. And as she does so she becomes aware of something in her peripheral vision – some indistinct shape, just over her shoulder. And she looks round to find that same strange girl, a little way off, watching. Just as she stood and watched last night.

Yuki lowers the photograph and stares at her. Then the girl slowly heads on over. Seems to simply float right through the heather. Instinctively, Yukiko gets to her feet – to meet her assailant – but gets up so fast that all the blood seems to drain from her head. She can feel it cascading over her shoulders. And the girl keeps on coming, with her hair, curly and blonde as a doll's, until she's right there, and Yuki can see her features. Can see how she doesn't smile. But reaches out, takes Yuki's hand and pulls it up towards her. Studies the photo, looks over at the water, and shakes her head.

You got the wrong reservoir, she says.

Yukiko only understands about half of what the girl is saying. So there's some confusion, before the girl finally takes Yuki's map, points at the same patch of blue to which Yuki's been clinging and says, You're here.

Then takes a moment to find a second location. Points at it, and says, That's where you want to be.

For a while Yukiko continues to stare at the map, as if it had contrived to trick her. Then the girl points up the hill, back where she came from. Takes a step or two, and beckons to Yuki, to suggest that she should accompany her. And Yuki thinks, Well, she seems to know what she's doing. So she tucks the photo in her jacket pocket and goes trotting after her.

The girl might be a little older than Yuki had first imagined. In her mid-teens, maybe. And as she's still a few steps ahead of her, Yuki keeps on looking at her incredible curly blonde hair. If you came to Japan, she wants to say, people would come over just to touch it. You'd have a queue right round the block.

At the brow of the hill they join a path which drops slowly down the other side and they're halfway along it when Yuki sees the motorbike leaning on its stand in the bottom of the valley. Not a particularly powerful-looking machine – the sort teenage boys ride, with thick-treaded wheels and a high-pitched engine – but the closer they get to it the more convinced Yuki is that it belongs to the girl and that she's going to expect Yuki to climb onto the back of it, which she's convinced is not such a great idea.

As they stumble down the path Yuki attempts to ask the girl, in her wretched English, how she knew where to find her, and several times the girl tries, and fails, to explain. Until, finally, she stops and mimes knocking at a door. And Yuki pictures this girl and the B & B Lady talking on the doorstep of the Grosvenor Hotel and the B & B Lady pointing out towards the moors.

Of course, what Yuki really wants to know is why the girl has taken such an interest in her. It's conceivable that she may just have been passing when Yuki crawled over the wall from the graveyard, but there was nothing arbitrary in her hanging about outside the B & B or showing up just now. There appears to be no easy way of broaching the subject. Yukiko's only thought is that she might appear to this blonde English girl as strange and exotic as the Brontës do to her.

The girl climbs onto the bike, kicks the stand back and with the toe of her other foot flicks out the kick-start. Jumps down on it, twice, before the engine catches, and pulls the throttle back hard a couple of times, to make sure it doesn't cut out. Then she looks over at Yuki, with the engine gently rattling, until she finally approaches. Yuki finds a footrest and swings her other leg over, as if she's mounting a horse. And since there's nowhere else to put them she places her hands on the girl's waist. Then the two of them go roaring down the path.

*

The girl seems to know how to handle the bike, following the path along the bottom of the valley with considerable care, but when at last they come up to the side of a tarmac road, she stops and looks long and hard in both directions before pulling back on the throttle with such ferocity that Yuki almost tumbles right off the seat.

As they fly down the road Yukiko thinks what a contrast this is to all the little capsules she's been travelling in lately. The wind blasts at her face and hair as if they're pushing through something solid. And Yuki looks down at the blur of road beneath her feet and wonders what condition she'd be in if she were to suddenly meet it, at such ridiculous speed.

Mercifully, within a couple of miles the bike is slowing down and pulling back off the road without them having passed more than a couple of cars coming the other way. This path is a little wider than the last one – more of a dirt track, with two furrows along it and a strip of grass in between – and seems to take them more directly where the girl wants to go. A couple of times she pulls up, to try and get her bearings. Then finally stops, kills the engine, flicks the stand down and, once she's sure that Yuki is with her, heads off up a steep slope.

The moment they clear the ridge and the water's spread out below them Yukiko can see how this is an altogether different proposition and recognises it as the location in her mother's photograph. The water seems closer to the sky somehow and there's a lot more of it. Down at one end, a stone pier runs out to some sort of small tower and Yuki finds that the tip of this construction appears at the edge of the photo, giving her something solid from which to orient herself.

She makes her way over to where her mother must have stood. Gets within a metre or so of it and glances at the photograph for confirmation. Then just stands and looks around.

The girl comes up alongside her. Asks to see the photo again and studies it pretty hard this time, as if now that they're here she might see something significant in it. Some monster about to loom out of the water or something just sinking out of sight.

She asks Yuki who took the photograph. Yuki pretends not to have understood, and the girl asks again, which gives Yuki a couple of moments in which to consider how she feels about answering the question honestly. She thinks, Well, she seems quite kind. Brought me all the way out here – to a place I would never have found on my own. So she takes the photos from her pocket, finds the one of her mother standing before the parsonage and hands it to the girl.

The girl looks at it. Then turns to Yukiko and says, Is that your mum?

Yukiko nods. The girl looks back at the photo. She says, And now she's dead. As if acknowledging it with her own small moment of consideration. Then looks up at Yuki. She died, she says.

Yukiko nods at the girl. Yes, she says.

For a while the two of them just stand and take in the

water and the moors around it. Yuki feels herself to be back in her mother's footsteps. And she sets off down towards the water – which looks black and viscous – apparently quite happy to leave the photos in the hands of the girl. Right on down to the water's edge, where she crouches. Trying to get her head low, so she can look right out over the water. Thinking of all the tiny vibrations and how this great block of water must consist of a million of them. Because what are waves – these little waves coming ashore at her feet – if not a manifestation of frequency?

She thinks all this and how things are now significantly different – and keeps finding herself drawn to one particular thought. Which is, If the girl wasn't here then I'd almost certainly do it. The thought slips away, then returns, like a small, rolling wave. And Yuki thinks, Well, in that case, I should do it anyway.

She takes a couple of steps back from the water, drops her rucksack and unzips her jacket. Pulls her fleece up over her head. Unbuttons her shirt, so that the wind strikes right onto her flesh now. Balances on one leg to take a shoe and sock off. Then the other. Unbuckles her belt and pulls down her trousers. Folds them twice and places them with the rest of her clothes, on top of her rucksack. Then heads for the water in her underwear.

She feels the last of the grass and heather beneath her feet, then dirt and small stones just before the water. Is hunched and tense before her feet are even wet. And when she does finally step into the water, just up to her ankles, it's so cold that a jolt of pain shoots up both legs and forms a knot in her stomach.

But she carries on, stepping carefully forward, and she's up to her knees before she turns back to the girl, just as she did half an hour ago. Wants to catch her eye – to let her know that there's nothing to be afraid of – but is forced to turn back and look out over the water to keep her balance.

When the water's up to her stomach it's as if her breath has been punched right out of her, and she thinks, Well, I may not be able to do this. My body may just lock up, refuse to work. And she can feel her heart clattering now, frantic, her lungs complaining. Then the water reaches her breasts and almost over her shoulders and her hands are numb just from reaching out into the water, for guidance and to stop herself tipping to one side. She thinks, It's not going to work unless I go right under. If I want to see her and understand where she's been all this time I have to go so far down that every hair on my head is wet. So she takes a breath – holds it in – and drops down under. And stays there, locked in the freezing cold, for a count of ten. Then fifteen. Twenty.

The girl has come right down to the water's edge, still holding the photographs. Stands and stares at the place where Yuki disappeared. The ripples continue to spread, like coils of rope. And as they spread out, the moors and their terrible silence seem to move on in.

Until, at last, Yuki comes up in a great rage. Back into the winter air. Wiping the water from her face. Locates the shore, with the girl standing there, waiting – and with her arms and legs already turning to stone, begins wading back towards her.

The moment Yukiko's skin is exposed to the air it begins to burn, and she wonders if this is what her mother experienced in her last few moments. She walks out of the reservoir, with the water still streaming from her and barely able to feel the small stones beneath her feet. And now the girl has hold of her elbow and is helping her over to her rucksack and her neat stack of clothes, as if she's just completed some marathon swim.

Before she reaches her clothes Yukiko realises she has nothing with which to dry herself and decides to sacrifice her fleece. She grabs it, wipes her face with it – drags it up and down each limb. Then pulls her trousers on over her damp legs, which are turning red now. Leaning against the girl, who she thinks must be pretty strong. Her shirt and jacket. But it's only when she sits on her rucksack to dry her feet and put her socks and shoes back on that Yuki really starts to shiver. All the same, she's thrilled. Feels she's really achieved something here. Although when she looks out at the water it's flat and dead again, as if her attempt to get in there and stir things up is already gone, forgotten, and the water's thoughts have turned back in on themselves.

In her first year at high school Yukiko fainted on two separate occasions. At the time she worried it was a habit her body might get into – something it might grow to like. Even now, in the right circumstances, she'll be convinced that whatever momentarily removed her from this world has finally managed to find her. That it's in her vicinity and about to throw its awful cloak back over her.

On the first occasion, she was standing in assembly. Mrs Muroya was up on stage, delivering some speech with that odd little stammer of hers, and Yuki remembers becoming aware of how many other girls were packed into the hall around her. Thinking that if there was a fire, say, or if she were to suddenly decide that she just wanted to get out of there, how much time it would take to get to the door. She continued to dwell on this, and even when she felt she'd dwelt on it sufficiently and would quite like to move on to something else, she found herself being drawn back to it, again and again, as if she'd started up some little inner motor that now refused to stop.

Then it was as if one of the girls over by the light switches started playing about with them. Yuki remembers thinking, Someone's going to get herself in trouble. And she was about to turn, to try and see what was going on back there, when something happened – as if something new and unusual had been introduced to her bloodstream. As if she was suddenly halfway back to the place where she did her dreaming. And the girl over at the light switches decided, Oh, what the hell, and turned the whole lot out.

When she came round Miss Ueno was crouched beside her looking, it has to be said, pretty irritated. Presumably, at the inconvenience of having to deal with this feeble little girl. She helped Yuki to her feet, then slowly led her through the others. It was good to see everyone give her so much space, though Yuki later concluded that they probably did this through some fear of contamination. Then she was led over to Miss Tanaka's office, where she was given a seat, a glass of water and all the time in the world to consider the complete weirdness of what had just gone on.

Two or three months later she passed out on the subway, which was even more troubling since she was among complete strangers and far from home. She remembers standing on the platform, the train pulling in and the doors slowly opening to reveal all the passengers squeezed inside. As she stepped into the carriage she looked down and noticed the thin strip of darkness between the train and the platform. And it was as if, having been acknowledged, that crazy darkness decided to come on up from under the train to be with her. She had just enough time to think, Hey,

I remember this from last time. Then she was gone.

When she came round, the train was rattling along between the stations, with Yuki being gently shaken from side to side and a bunch of people staring down at her. The fact that the train was moving seemed incomprehensible to her. Surely, she thought, if I've fallen apart and ceased to function, then the rest of the world should have ceased to function too.

The next morning her mother took her to see the doctor. He asked her three or four rather mundane questions and took her blood pressure (which he noted was a little low) but his general attitude seemed to be that girls Yuki's age were prone to over-excitement and occasional fainting and that her most important consideration should be to ensure she had a decent breakfast before venturing out into the world, or risk surrendering herself to more blackouts in the weeks to come.

There have been plenty of times since, when she's been stressed or emotional, and she's worried that she was about to go back under. But some telling element was always missing: a bitterness at the tip of her tongue . . . some vague sense of a fizzing, electrical aura. And, not least, the girl over by the light switches, threatening to get herself into trouble again.

Now she's got her clothes back on Yuki's hoping she's going to start feeling a little warmer but her teeth are chattering and she can feel her shirt and trousers getting damp against her underwear. She thinks maybe moving about might generate a little heat so she pulls her rucksack up onto her back and marches up and down. Then she and the girl decide to head back and they're halfway down the steep bank when the girl grabs Yuki's arm and says she has an idea and knows exactly where they should go.

They drive out along the same track they came in on, but when they reach the road the girl pulls them round to the left and they race along it for a couple of minutes, then turn onto a wider road and follow that for a while. Yuki's hair cracks and flaps in the wind. She thinks, Maybe she's trying to dry me out by taking me up and down the roads of Northern England. She spots the garage up ahead before the girl starts slowing down for it – nothing more than a forecourt with a couple of cars filling up. But as they near it she sees the cafe beyond it – a bright block of light, a little like an American diner, but wider, with a luminous sign around the edge of the roof.

All that light looks pretty warm and inviting. They park the bike and climb the steps, but instead of turning left towards the cafe the girl leads Yuki down a corridor and into the women's bathroom where she rests a hand on top of an old-fashioned hand-drier, about the same size as a small refrigerator, as if she's modelling it at a hand-drier fair. Waves Yuki over, then hits the big silver disc on the front and the thing starts chugging and whirring away.

It takes a while to reach its full capacity but once it's going it's like standing next to a DC-10. Yuki dips her hand under, to check the temperature. Then bows and slowly moves in towards the jet of hot air, as if inserting her head into a lion's mouth. It feels pretty good. She drops her head a little, to avoid actually setting her hair on fire, and has just about found the optimum distance when the motor cuts out. But before she looks up the girl hits the big silver button and the motor starts clanking and whirring away again.

It seems like they could be here for quite a while so Yuki slips off her rucksack and squats down on it so that her blouse billows in and out as the jet of hot air flies down her back. The girl leans against the drier and gives it a clank every time it cuts out, while Yukiko moves on from drying her hair to drying different parts of her clothing. At some point, a woman in a suit comes in – looks over at them, but just kind of ignores them. As if she sees this kind of thing all the time. Fixes herself up in the mirror, then strolls back out.

After five minutes Yukiko's feeling pretty dry and a

whole lot warmer. She has a look in the mirror and finds her hair has gone super-static. She tries patting it down, but it just drifts back up, like she's got a hold of a Van der Graaff generator. So in the end she gives up and the two of them head for the door.

They walk on down to the cafe and take a seat next to the window. All the tables and chairs are fixed to the floor and made from the same moulded red plastic. At the end of the day, Yuki thinks, they probably just clear away all the dishes and hose the whole place down.

Yukiko does her best to tell the girl that she'll pay for the food, and that she should order whatever she wants. The menu actually has tiny photographs of what each meal looks like, which immediately bumps the place up in Yuki's estimation. She orders a tea and a slice of apple tart, and the girl orders a tea and cake.

They're sitting and staring out at the heavy sky when the girl says, You're Japanese, aren't you? Yuki nods and the girl tells her how they get a lot of Japanese visitors because of the Brontës. Yuki wants to say, I'm not like all the loonies. How hers is more of an investigative/spiritual visit, to do with her dead mother, but thinks there's every chance the girl's already worked that out for herself. So she just looks back out at the sky and remembers what it felt like to go right under the freezing water. To have the water seal itself over her head and to be momentarily lost down there.

The food and drinks arrive and the two of them attempt to have a conversation. Yuki asks the girl if she shouldn't maybe be in school but the girl shakes her head with such conviction – almost affronted – that she decides to leave it at that. Yuki's still picking away at her pie when the girl asks if she can have another look at the photos. So Yuki takes the envelope out of her rucksack and hands her the one of her mother outside the parsonage. The girl leans in and studies it hard. And, perhaps to try and avoid having to talk about her mother, Yuki hands her the photo of the wind-bent tree and asks if she recognises it.

The girl frowns as she keeps on looking at it. She's pretty sure she's seen it, she says, but is having trouble remembering where. And for a while Yukiko watches her, appreciating all that teenage concentration. Then asks, very quietly, if she has a sister. The girl looks up and Yuki has to repeat the question a couple of times before she understands. She shakes her head. She has a brother, she says, and nods in the direction of the motorbike. And Yukiko sees how the bike must belong to an older brother, who quite likely has no idea his kid sister is out on it now, ferrying some Jap girl between possible psychic hotspots – and wonders how he might feel about this, if he knew.

They've almost finished eating when the girl says, Hey, and points out of the window. A few flakes of snow are falling – tiny outriders of some greater, yet gentle invasion. They both stop and stare for a couple of moments. Yuki's sure she must have spent half her life thinking about snow, but when it starts, even now, it's still magical, bewildering. Each snowflake skating along its own invisible plane – circuitous, as if searching for a particular place to land.

Over the last four or five years Yukiko has read more about snow, its origins and its consequences than she could have imagined, not least the work of Ukichiro Nakaya. But though his research into the formation of snow crystals was pretty extensive he seemed to take very little interest in what happens to them as they fall. As far as Yukiko's concerned a snow crystal has, in its brief existence, three significant periods: (i) its formation, way up in the ether, (ii) its actual descent, usually clustered together with other crystals in the form of a flake, and (iii) its existence after it has landed, among billions of other snow crystals. It seems to Yuki that a snow crystal is most itself in the second of these three stages, as it ranges through the air – sometimes sideways, sometimes back towards the heavens – in that stunning piece of collective theatre. Merrily eccentric and silent as the grave.

Yukiko pays and the two of them head back out into the cold. The snow has stopped, leaving a fine white dust across the ground, and as they pull away the bike's tyres cut cleanly through it, revealing the road, black and wet beneath. The girl tells Yuki her name is Denny and that she thinks she may know where to find the bent-over tree – which she believes may have been struck by lightning. And as they fly along, Yuki thinks how she'd like to organise an exhibition of lightning-struck objects, each one mangled and dumbfounded in its own individual way.

They're on the main road a little longer this time before pulling off onto another dirt track, which they wind along for half a mile or so. Then Denny stops, rests the bike on its stand and leads Yukiko up a rocky gulley, which slowly swings round to the right and finally comes out into a tiny valley, similar to the one with the Brontë Sitting Stone and Daydreaming Bridge in it. Yuki follows Denny, quite content to have someone else take the lead for a while, and they're halfway up the valley when Denny suddenly stops, raises her arm and points off to the right. And once Yuki comes up alongside her

113

and looks where Denny's pointing she sees the sheep's bloody remains.

They walk slowly over towards it, as if taking care not to disturb the scene of a crime. The ribs reach up out of the meat. Some of the intestines are strewn over the ground, the wool smeared with blood. The sheep's head is untouched and turned to one side, as if to look away from the dreadful things being done to it.

Denny peers in at the guts, still wet, and says that this must've happened in the last hour or so. Then she turns and studies the ridge above them. Takes Yuki by the arm and leads her quickly, quietly away.

At the top of the bank Denny drops down and pulls on Yuki's sleeve till she crouches beside her. Tells her not to move. Then she scuttles away – back towards the motorbike, but straight over the moor this time, rather than along the gulley, running with her head down, as if there might be snipers training their sights on her. Yuki watches as she grows smaller and smaller, reaches another ridge, then drops down over it. Keeps on watching – occasionally glancing around in every other direction, without quite knowing what she might be looking out for. Until finally Denny reappears, just along from where Yuki last saw her, and starts heading back across the moors.

She's out of breath when she finally squats back down beside Yukiko, but is fairly beaming. She slips a hand inside her jacket and pulls out something bulky, wrapped in an oily rag. Peels back the cloth, one corner at a time, until a gun is revealed – right there in her hand. A jet-black pistol. She looks up at Yuki, smiles and hands it to her.

It's heavy, like a lump of solid steel. Above the barrel is a second, narrower barrel. The handle, cross-hatched on both sides, is rough against Yuki's palm. And as she stares at it Denny dips her hand into her jacket pocket and pulls out half a dozen metal pellets – picks one out, between finger and thumb, and takes the pistol back from Yuki.

She flips a catch. Lifts the upper barrel so that it pivots at the tip. Pulls it back, straining as she does so, until it clicks and settles, inserts a pellet, then folds the barrel back into place.

Yukiko has never been especially keen on guns, even in the movies. The one in Denny's hand may be little more than an air pistol, but you don't make a gun that heavy and apparently powerful without intending it to hurt or possibly kill someone.

Denny lifts her head, sizing up the landscape, then crawls over to a large flat rock which juts out over the valley. Yukiko follows, pulling her rucksack along beside her, until they're both peering over the edge. Denny tells Yuki she thinks it's either a dog or maybe a wolf that killed the sheep and that their arrival may have scared it away. She nods towards the bloody carcass. There's still plenty of meat left on it, she says.

Yuki stares down at the sheep, then round at Denny. We're going to see if it comes back? she says.

Denny nods.

Yuki looks a little incredulous.

And we're going to shoot it?

Denny smiles and nods again.

Yukiko looks up the valley. Tries to picture a dog creeping back towards the bloody sheep. What if Denny shoots and misses? What if she hits the dog but it's not quite killed?

But Denny seems to be settling herself down for a sustained period of waiting, and Yuki knows that she's not going to get back to the B & B without the girl. So she tries to make herself comfortable and for a while they both lie with their chins resting on their forearms. He's coming back, Denny says. I know he is.

As they lie there Yukiko can feel the cold from the rock reach right up into her. Denny lifts the gun, closes one eye and tracks up and down the valley. Then puts it to one side and rests her face against her crossed hands.

Your mum, she says. Did she die a long time ago?

Yukiko nods. Thinks, Ten years sounds like such a long old time, but most days she's right there with me.

And did she die in England?

Yuki shakes her head. In Japan.

For a while they gaze out over the valley. Then Yuki studies the clouds above the horizon, trying to work out whether it's likely to snow again.

A minute or two later Yukiko reaches over and carefully takes the gun. Examines it, then holds it out before her, with one eye closed, just as Denny did. She sweeps it up and down the length of the valley. Picks out the sheep, still dead, and considers pulling the trigger. Thinks, What the hell am I doing – lying on a rock in England in the middle of winter, contemplating shooting a dead sheep? This cannot be a healthy way to be.

She puts the gun down. You said a wolf, she says.

Denny turns to her – doesn't understand.

Yuki says, Said it could be a wolf. What's a *wolf*?

Denny has a think. Then explains how a wolf is like a regular dog, but wilder. One that lives out in the fields and trees.

Yukiko is beginning to wish she hadn't asked.

Mostly up in Scotland, Denny says. But some of them get this far south in the winter – when there aren't that many people about.

Yukiko stares down into the valley. Then she turns and reaches for her rucksack, takes out her notebook, finds an empty page and passes the book and pen over to Denny.

Well, OK, Denny says. But I'm not much good at drawing.

She gathers her thoughts for a moment, then begins to outline a simple profile, with a rectangular head, pointy snout, broad haunch and shoulder, a tapered waist and a scrawny tail. She adds a single triangular ear, a mean oval eye and a zig-zag of sharp teeth along the open mouth. Makes a dozen or so individual scratches to represent its fur. Then looks at her work – apparently quite pleased – and slides the book back over to Yukiko.

She asks if these British wolves have ever been known to attack people.

Oh, sure, Denny says. And she tells Yukiko about a woman who was walking along the edge of the moors one evening maybe four or five years ago and how a wolf grabbed her by the coat and dragged her off into the darkness.

Yuki says, And she was killed?

Denny nods enthusiastically. All they found was her coat with a few old bones in it.

Yukiko whistles, tucks her notebook back into her rucksack and the two of them look back down into the valley with the dead sheep lying in it.

Yuki can feel the cold begin to take a firmer grip of her. But, despite this, she rests her head on her arm and closes her eyes. She thinks about wolves, where they might live – in secret caves and moorland tunnels – and whether they're ever tempted to creep into the villages, after food from the garbage, or to snack on domestic pets. She's slipping steadily towards sleep when she gets a nudge in the ribs. And she lifts her head to find Denny pointing the gun up to the top of the valley. It takes Yuki a second or two to spot the dog trotting down the path – a large, thick-haired creature, and not a breed with which she's familiar. Perhaps something between a dog and a wolf. But with its nose down, sweeping the ground and its head full of its own powerful imaginings – pausing here and there to sweep and sniff with more intensity, then moving on. Its mouth hangs open, and even from this distance Yuki can see how it is in possession of quite a set of teeth. If Denny does decide to take a shot at it Yuki sincerely hopes the animal is killed outright, or so comprehensively incapacitated that it won't come bounding after them.

Twenty metres from the sheep Yuki and Denny see how the dog suddenly stops and locks onto something. Turns sharply and is drawn right up to the carcass as if on a track. And in a second it has its head right in among all the bones and gore, tail flapping. About as happy as a dog can be.

Denny has one eye closed now, with both arms out at full stretch. Yuki looks down, thinking, No, not a wolf. Ears and snout not sufficiently pointy. And, given the thickness of its fur, she wonders if Denny's gun will make much of an impression. But the more the dog dips its head into the sheep's blood and bones, the more Yukiko finds herself thinking, Just do it. Just shoot the damned dog.

Then, out of nowhere, three or four voices come rattling down the valley. Women chatting and laughing. Denny and Yuki look back up the path to see a group of six women blundering into view. English women, but not much younger than Yuki's own Elders. The same new boots. The same determined heartiness. Their waterproof trousers flapping like flags around their ageing limbs.

They're halfway down the valley before one of them spots the dog at the sheep and alerts the others. And suddenly there's a terrible commotion, and one woman bursts through, shouting, with a dog's lead swinging from her hand. She makes a grab for the dog – for its collar – but the smell of the sheep's blood has filled its head right up. So that each time she makes a lunge for it, it jerks back, skips around the carcass and plunges back in from the other side.

Denny and Yuki are finding the whole thing more than a little irritating. Just a couple of minutes ago there had been peace and quiet, and the prospect of a wolf to be shot at. But the likelihood of that near-mystical experience has been driven away by these stupid women running around and bumping into each other in their stupid boots and rucksacks.

As Yuki looks on she's vaguely aware of Denny slowly withdrawing, but decides to have one last glance before going after her. The woman has the dog by the collar now, but the creature's so excited it's yanking her every which way.

Yuki thinks, Don't English people bother to train their dogs?

She turns to leave, but instead of seeing Denny creeping off across the moors, Yuki finds her standing right beside her, with the gun at arm's length pointing down into the valley, with one eye tightly shut.

If she'd had the time Yuki might've asked if she was sure this was such a good idea. But she sees Denny grit her teeth and narrow her open eye a little. Hears a 'schtack', sees the gun recoil and Denny's arm kick back with it.

A terrible shriek comes up from the valley. Yukiko

turns and looks. The woman with the dog has her back to Yuki and Denny, but is standing straight as a post, clutching her backside. Yuki ducks down, expecting Denny to do the same. But Denny just stands on the rock, defiant, with the pistol hanging from her hand.

Below, half the women are fussing and flapping while the rest turn to see where the shot came from. The woman clutching her ass pushes the others aside and looks up. Stares at Denny, who's laughing now. And the more the woman stares, indignant, the harder Denny laughs.

Yuki is still trying to come to terms with the fact that Denny actually shot the woman when Denny says, C'mon. And when she looks over her shoulder Denny is gone – flying over the heather, back towards the bike. Yuki stumbles to her feet and grabs her rucksack, so now all the women in the valley get a good old look at her. She sees the woman who got shot lift her hand from her ass and point right up at her. Her other hand still has a hold of the dog's collar. She keeps her eyes on Yuki, but drops her head towards the dog. Says something like, Go on, boy – get 'em. Then lets it go.

For the first twenty metres or so Yuki's still trying to get the rucksack up onto her shoulders. Then she just gives up and carries it by the straps, so that it clatters against her thigh as she charges along.

Denny is a pretty good runner, but halfway back to the ridge she stops and rests her hands on her knees, which allows Yuki to catch her up. As Yuki comes alongside she sees that she's stopped not because she's out of breath but because she's laughing so hard. Then Yuki looks back and sees the dog clamber up onto the rock where they've just been lying. Sees that big head turn with its ears up, sharp – find them, then set off after them.

No one's laughing as they race across that last stretch of heather. At the ridge Yuki allows herself another quick glance over her shoulder. The dog's still thundering in their direction. Has already managed to halve the distance between them. Then she and Denny go scrambling down towards the bike.

They both trip and fall on the slope – it's impossible to do otherwise. They join the track at the bottom, and for those last few steps before they reach the bike they can hear the dog barking somewhere behind them. Yuki has to wait for Denny to climb on. Desperately wants to join her, but knows she won't be able to start the bike with her on the seat. Denny flips the lever out. Kicks it once . . . twice . . . with the dog at the foot of the slope now. Kicks it a third time before the engine catches. Then pulls back on the throttle, hard.

Get the fuck on, she says.

The bike pulls away before Yuki is properly settled. The dog is right down the path now and hammering along behind. So when Yuki does finally drop onto the seat the fact that Denny is pulling so hard on the throttle brings the front wheel up off the ground and throws Yuki backwards. And, for what feels like an hour, they seem to float along on that back wheel. Seem to have entered their own slow and silent world. Until finally Denny releases the throttle long enough to bring the front wheel back into contact with the ground. And at that moment – when the dream suddenly seems to evaporate and the motorbike bursts back into reality – Yukiko sees the dog's great head come up alongside her, its snout all clotted with blood. She wants not to look, but its eyes glint up at her. Its ears fold back, its lips peel away from that great row of teeth. Then it lunges towards her and takes a nip.

From that point on the dog is falling behind them. Perhaps it feels it has achieved what it set out to do. And the more the bike pulls away the less inclined it seems to pursue them. Until finally it lollops to a halt. And the last time Yukiko sees it, it's standing in the middle of the path watching them go.

They rattle on between the hills until Denny's quite sure they're clear of danger. Drops the throttle back and over her shoulder asks Yuki if she's OK. But it's only when she pulls up and turns right around that she has any idea just how upset Yuki is. Yuki waves her forward – telling her to keep on going. So they carry on for another few hundred metres. But even then, as Yuki does her best to explain how the dog managed to bite her, she keeps on glancing back down the path, expecting to see the dog charging towards them, determined to get its teeth into her again.

There's a small rip in Yukiko's trousers, high up on her thigh, and by shifting the material back and forth she's able to locate four small punctures, each brimming with blood.

We should go back and bloody well kill it, says Denny, though neither she nor Yuki expects them to do any such thing. Then Denny quizzes Yuki about tetanus jabs – whether she's had one lately. But all Yuki wants to do is get back to her room and try to forget this ever happened. Get off this damned moor and never come out here again.

A quarter of a mile or so short of Haworth Denny parks the bike at the side of the road, flips the seat up and tucks the pistol into a secret little compartment there. Then the two of them head into town, with Denny carrying Yuki's rucksack and Yuki limping alongside her. The first few houses have just come into view when the snow starts to fall again, a little more heavily now, and by the time they reach the steps of the Grosvenor Hotel the air is thick with it and the whole world feels as if it's shut right down.

Yukiko sometimes has trouble remembering how she felt about snow before the death of her mother. She assumes that, like most other children, she admired its powers of disruption and transformation and considered it great material with which to play. Even now, despite what it did to her mother and, indeed, how it fucked up her entire family, she doesn't resent or particularly fear it. She's simply a little more inclined to take it seriously.

It must be five or six years since she first heard of Ukichiro Nakaya and his snow experiments, although she didn't get her hands on *Snow Crystals: Natural and Artificial* till she was at college and managed to track down a copy in the library. Nakaya is sometimes credited with compiling the first general classification of snow crystals, and indeed one page of the book has each fundamental type laid out in a grid, like a sort of periodic table of snow. But Yuki knows, even from her own amateur investigations, that Suzuki Bokushi created a similar chart a hundred years earlier, in *Snow Country Tales*. No, the reason Yuki is so in awe of Ukichiro Nakaya is that he approached snow with the same intelligence and rigour you'd expect of any scientist, and along the way worked out what conditions influence each crystal's design.

She's no idea how many years he devoted to snow analysis before attempting to create his own artificial crystal. There are photographs of him out in the snow up Mount Tokachi, bent over a microscope, and to this day Yuki can't conceive how you take a crystal, fix it to a slide and tuck it under the eyepiece while keeping it intact. He had assistants, Yukiko knows this. Quite possibly a whole team of snow-folk eager to serve him in any useful way. But when she pictures him going about his icy business she prefers to think of him out there on his own – monastic, as befits a man contemplating something as delicate, as ethereal as snow.

The first time she opened up *Snow Crystals* in one of the study cubicles at the university she all but squawked, like a goddamned bird or something. The book contains some text and a fair number of graphs and tables, but most of it just consists of hundreds of microscopic photographs of snow crystals, half a dozen to a page. In hindsight, she should maybe have limited herself to a couple of pages on that first encounter. Allowed herself to be blown away by the weird mechanical beauty and the astounding symmetry, before returning the book to the shelves – and come back, refreshed and psychically rested, the following day. But she turned the page to find another dozen, even more ornate and viciously barbed creations, all sprouting from the same hexagonal core. So that by the time she turned the page a second, third and fourth time she was inundated, and what had seemed incredible a minute earlier became so strange as to be practically meaningless.

She had to leave her cubicle and walk about, to try and clear her head a little. But even as she did so, with all those peculiar shapes jangling around her, she couldn't help but marvel at the fact that their only component was plain water, extravagantly spun way up in the clouds.

The astonishing variety was, in part, what drove Nakaya to attempt to create his own crystals – the fact that the sky was apparently capable of casting out an infinite range, all perfectly and elegantly fashioned. It forced him in from the cold, into his mountainside laboratory, where, ironically, he had to replicate the freezing conditions he'd just left behind. Yuki read somewhere that he'd zip himself into an old flying suit to keep himself warm. She's heard how astronomers in the Fifties and Sixties also wore them – some of them heated, and trailing electric wires – since an astronomer is busiest in the long, dark nights of winter and once the roof of the observatory is opened up, well you're pretty much out of doors. Yukiko delights in the fact that pilots, astronomers and snow researchers have all worn the same strange suits – entirely different disciplines, but all preoccupied with the sky and what goes on up there.

Sooner or later Nakaya must have grasped that the only way to observe a crystal in mid-formation was to try and cultivate his own. So he got himself a cloud chamber and set about doing just that. The problem he had was replicating the conditions that would normally occur in mid-air, so he threaded all sorts of string and filaments through the chamber to try and give the nascent crystals something on which to grab a hold. It was only by accident, the story goes (and Yuki has noted how it is often an accident that operates at a tale's significant moment – an accident, in this instance, being another name for Fate) that a rabbit hair off the hood of Nakaya's coat found its way into the chamber. So that when he next peered in he saw the beginnings of a crystal, perched on the tip of that rabbit hair. Something about its texture offered the crystal the necessary traction, when all the previous lengths of thread and twine had been too smooth or knobbly – or not smooth or knobbly enough.

There is cine footage – Nakaya's own, Yuki thinks – of the work that followed. Time-lapse sequences of these microscopic forces exploding, in eight different directions. Then even closer/more magnified footage of the growth of a single branch of ice, like a rocket nudging through the upper atmosphere. And if seeing microscopic photographs of crystals in all their glory isn't mind-blowing enough, then seeing footage of one taking shape, wilful and sinister, will probably do it. On first encountering the film, Yuki was reminded of her own junior snow experiments – how amateur they were in comparison (she was only young, after all, with no major funding) but also how hers were doing quite the opposite, since Nakaya was attempting to replicate this most incredible act of creation, whilst hers were nothing but reduction of the bluntest kind.

Having created the circumstances necessary to cultivate a crystal, Nakaya found that altering the temperature and saturation in the chamber encouraged the crystals to assume different forms. The colder the conditions in the chamber the less ornate the crystal. There were moments, as Yuki sat in her own small cubicle, when she'd think, I've ploughed through all this stuff, hoping to get to grips with snow and maybe somehow dismantle, even *disarm* it. But the deeper I go the more threatening it appears. Through a microscope's lens most things start to look a little alien, but a snow crystal is like something from a sci-fi nightmare – looks positively murderous.

Then, when she felt she was just about done with Nakaya, a friend put her in touch with someone at Kobe University who was carrying out some real, academic research into the man. They exchanged polite emails and the researcher eventually mentioned that he had a short clip of Nakaya being interviewed in his laboratory in the early 1950s. Unfortunately, the accompanying sound was missing, but the researcher said he'd had the footage digitised and that he'd happily send it over to Yuki, on condition that she promised not to copy it or show it to anyone else. She agreed, and a couple of days later a small package arrived with a memory stick, wrapped in a typed note. Yuki imagines the researcher hearing, through their mutual acquaintance, how her mother had died in the snow and how she's since become something of a snow-maniac. That this was her way of trying to come to terms with her mother's death, etc. Either way, she felt honoured to have the footage, despite the fact that it was only two or three minutes long – footage that practically no one beyond Nakaya's family and close colleagues had ever seen.

As soon as she found the package in her pigeonhole she went straight up to her room and loaded it onto her computer. And there he was, in black and white, sitting in his mountainside laboratory, with a sheepskin hat on his head and the flaps down over his ears, apparently talking quite earnestly, with the warmth of his words turning to steam before his face. Yukiko assumes that he was discussing his work, not least because at various points he'd turn and nod towards different corners of the laboratory. But for most of the short film he talked straight to the camera – as if he might have set it up and started it running himself. So that his solitariness, which is of such peculiar importance to Yuki, might be maintained.

She doesn't particularly mind the fact she's no idea what he's saying. Watching someone talk without the sound makes you appreciate their facial expressions – particularly, what they do with their eyes. There are two or three moments in the film when Nakaya looks so intently into the camera that Yukiko really does feel that he is addressing himself quite specifically to her. And on more than one occasion she's been inclined to think that his words, if she could only hear them, would turn out to be a message, or some sort of explanation. A personal apology, on behalf of the snow.

Yuki finds her key and leads Denny on up to her bedroom. Hasn't had the chance to properly examine her leg yet, so she sits on the bed, moves her trousers from side to side again and presses down on either side of the bite, as if trying to purge herself of venom – of the memory of the dog getting its teeth into her. The frayed rips in her trousers are blood-soaked and she's having trouble seeing what's going on so she stands, undoes her belt. Then hesitates. Denny shrugs. Says, Go ahead. So Yuki eases her trousers down over the wound. The blood has already started to congeal in the four neat holes, and the neighbouring skin is beginning to bruise. Denny leans in. Asks if it hurts. Yukiko nods her head two or three times. She seems kind of bewildered. Has never been bitten by a dog before.

They're both still looking at the bite when Yuki asks Denny why she did it. Why she shot the woman. Denny thinks for a while. I just couldn't resist it, she says. And starts to laugh again, but not half so hard now, or for half as long.

It feels to Yuki that her leg has been kicked rather than bitten. The muscle beneath the cut is growing tight and aches like mad. She sits back on the bed and sees the dog's head easing up beside her, as if it just wanted some attention – a stroke, or a chuck under the chin. Can feel its hot breath against her leg, for that single second . . . see its ears flatten . . . its eye roll back and look up at her . . . its big mouth parting . . . it leaning in and taking a nip at her.

Denny's wandering around the room now, looking at Yuki's belongings on the chest of drawers and hanging over chairs, while Yuki continues to gently prod at her thigh. Here and there Denny stops to have a closer look at a book . . . a blouse . . . Yuki's Japanese toothpaste. Then turns and tells Yuki that if she really doesn't want to see a doctor, she should at least get some cream and clean things up a bit. Yukiko doesn't argue. And after a little more looking around Denny takes the keys from the bedside table and heads out into town.

Yukiko can hear the front door being pulled to and Denny's feet on the steps below the window. She carefully lifts her legs and slips them beneath the covers. Wonders what would have happened if she'd fallen off the bike as they tried to get away. Imagines the dog tearing her to pieces – her disappearing into a small storm of shredded flesh and clothing, like the scene when the Brontë Father chopped up Charlotte's clothes. And she's half asleep fifteen minutes later when Denny returns, with snow on both her shoulders and a takeaway coffee in each hand.

Denny fills the sink with hot soapy water and dips the facecloth in it. Yuki perches on the edge of the bed and once the blood's been cleaned away the two of them have another good look at it. It's not a huge wound, but as Denny says, you really don't want any extra holes in you if you can possibly help it. She opens the tube of ointment and smears the thick white cream over the bite marks – can feel the punctures beneath her fingertips as she smoothes it in.

Denny says, Damn. I should've bought some plasters. Then stands and looks around the room. Yuki doesn't understand what she's talking about, but Denny asks for directions to the bathroom and returns with some toilet tissue, folds it twice and places it over the wound. She hands Yuki her coffee and a packet of paracetamol, kicks off her own shoes and climbs up onto the bed.

Yuki takes the Brontë biscuits from the bedside table and she and Denny are working their way through them when Denny looks round the room at the drawers, the dressing table, the little sink in the corner and says, This place kind of gives me the creeps.

Yuki has a look herself. Other than the hotel room in Leeds and Kumiko's, it's the only place she's slept since she got here. She was beginning to think maybe it wasn't so strange.

When she's finished her coffee Denny asks if she can look at Yuki's notebook – the one in which Yuki asked her to draw a wolf. So Yukiko takes it out of her rucksack, hands it to Denny and sits and watches, to see what she makes of it.

The book is pretty evenly split between text and

sketches. Quite a few of the drawings appear to be ideas for eccentric clothing: vast-collared capes . . . futuristic hats . . . platform boots with secret compartments. Scattered through the book are various unusual haircuts. In one sketch a woman's hair is swept up into a towering beehive, with a miniature camera hidden in it. Yuki explains that it's for a project in which she secretly photographs people's reactions to her own spectacular haircut, but isn't sure Denny quite grasps what she means.

There are seating plans for retro spacecraft . . . cross-sections of residences with rooftop helipads and subterranean swimming pools . . . a still life of a pair of laceless trainers . . . mediaeval monsters. Denny works her way through the book, flipping forwards and backwards until she reaches the end. Then starts again, this time looking more closely at Yuki's handwriting. She points quite randomly at a piece of text and asks Yuki to translate it. Some are just odd little thoughts – poetic, philosophical. Some are quotes from books she's read.

Denny watches Yuki's fingers as she translates four or five sentences before appreciating that not only do the lines run from top to bottom, they advance from right to left. She takes the book from Yuki and holds it out before her.

She says, So the front of a book in England is the back of a book in Japan?

Yukiko nods.

Denny is still digesting this when Yuki's phone starts

ringing. Yuki picks it up, checks the screen to see who's calling, and places it carefully back down on the bed.

My sister, she says.

Then she and Denny sit and watch the phone ringing, as if it's some strange creature that's just stirred from hibernation. Until at last it stops. And the room is somehow filled with Yuki's sister's resentment at Yuki not having taken her call.

When Yuki finally looks up Denny asks how long it is since her mother stayed in Haworth. Yuki holds up the fingers and thumbs on both hands.

Ten years? says Denny. She can see how just talking about her mother upsets Yukiko. Sees how her eyes are beginning to prickle with tears. All the same, Yuki reaches back over to her rucksack, takes out her precious pack of photos and carefully lays them out on the bed. There's her mother outside the parsonage . . . the reservoir . . . the bent-over tree. And now she adds the photo of her mother by the Grosvenor's front steps and the small table by the open window. Denny squints down at the last photo. Then looks up at the window next to the sink.

She stayed here? she says, pointing at the bed on which they're both sitting. Yukiko shakes her head and points at the wall, beyond the tiny TV and chest of drawers.

Next door? says Denny. Your mum stayed in the room next door?

Yukiko nods and gives her a little smile.

Denny slides off the bed and takes two or three steps

towards it. Turns. She wants to know if Yuki has managed to get in there yet. Yuki says that she hasn't. So Denny goes over to the window, opens it up and leans right out, to see if there's any way of creeping along to the next window. When she pulls her head back in her hair is flecked with snow.

She drags the sash back down and Yuki watches as she tries to work out how they might contrive to find their way in there. Watches her stare at the threadbare carpet, thinking – just as Yuki thought earlier – that maybe there's a way of crawling through, under the floor.

Yukiko waits a while – perhaps because she knows where it will lead – then mentions, super-casually, how she's seen some keys downstairs, near the kitchen. And that she's pretty sure that one of the keys is for the room next door.

Denny opens her palms out wide and shrugs her shoulders. Well, what the fuck are we waiting for?

Yuki digs out some clean trousers but has trouble pulling them on because her leg won't bend as much as it should do. Plus she's trying to keep the dressing in place. She finds some socks and shoes, then she and Denny slip out onto the landing and tiptoe along to the next room. They stand beside the door in silence, listening. Denny crouches down and peers through the keyhole. Takes a grip of the door handle and turns it. The door's still locked.

OK, she whispers. So where's this key?

They creep down the stairs and stand in the hallway

for a minute among all the leaflets, trying to hear if anyone's about. Then on into the dining room and over to the door to the kitchen. It's Denny who finally pushes it open – wide enough for them both to see inside.

There's a faint sound, but way off in the distance. Somebody talking – or maybe a TV or radio, with the sound down low. Yuki is hoping Denny might volunteer to creep in and take the keys off the hook. It was Denny, after all, who recently shot a woman in the ass. She seems to be quite naturally wayward. But it's not Denny who's searching for some psychic trace of her mother – some tiny, telling vibration that may lead to greater, more significant information and help her comprehend what happened ten years ago. So Yukiko steels herself and slips past Denny. Tiptoes over and reaches up to the hook below the number 6. Lifts the keys with such care there's barely any contact between the ring and the hook. And the moment she has them in her fist, she turns and limps off at speed – past Denny and over towards the stairs.

She's tempted to head straight back to her room, lock the door and lie on the bed till she's recovered – so that she can be 100% sure she's not about to have a heart attack. But by the time she reaches the landing she's thinking, Better to carry on. To get into the room and return the keys as soon as possible.

Denny's standing right beside her as she slips the key into the lock. They stop and listen one last time. Then Yuki turns the key. She feels the mechanism resist, then accommodate it and surrender. She takes hold of the handle, twists it and finally the door gives way to her.

The room is pristine – the bed neatly made, every surface clean and empty. Yuki's first thought is, They've kept it like this in my mother's honour. The room is now a museum to her. Like Charlotte and Emily's rooms in the parsonage. A sacred place.

It's pretty much a mirror image of her own room, if a fraction smaller. The same decor, with the sink and fireplace up against the same shared wall. When they close the door it's a little dark so Denny turns on the lamp on the bedside table, which casts a soft light over the bed, making it seem even more hallowed. Then she heads on into the room, so that she and Yuki are standing on either side of the bed. The room is suddenly still, as if all the air has been sucked right out – through the drain in the sink . . . the gap along the base of the skirting board . . . the plug sockets. Denny's staring at the bed – at its impossible smoothness. She slowly reaches out a hand to touch it. To sweep her palm across its cold, flat sheets. But Yuki says, No – before she even knows it. And finds that she's raised her hand, palm up, like a traffic cop.

I'm sorry. I'm sorry, she says. Then shakes her head.

Yuki is beginning to appreciate how little thought she's devoted to what she'd do if she ever managed to get in here. It would appear, judging by her own strange behaviour, that she doesn't want anything to be disturbed. So she stands and waits and listens – in that dead, empty space, with that vacant bed before her. Keeps on waiting, with Denny standing across from her.

She tries to remember what she was like at twelve or thirteen, when her mother was over here. Her preoccupations. She remembers talking to her mother as she packed her suitcase. She and Kumi being driven over to their grandparents. Grandma Hisako taking her into the guest bedroom. Her own lonely bed.

Then she remembers that terrible dread at both her parents being away, halfway round the planet. Feels something quicken. As if aware of something closing in on her. And another lock turns. A door swings slowly open. And all her mother-love comes suddenly rushing up in her again.

Poor Yukiko drops to her knees, with her hands on the bed's cover, soft and kind. And suddenly crying. With her mother gone – gone and so very far away.

Denny stands and watches. She feels that she should go over, but thinks Yuki might just want to cry and remember her mother on her own. So she continues to stand and watch. And after a while Yuki lifts her head. I'm sorry, she says again. Always apologising. And finally manages to catch her breath, as if a little air has found its way back into the room.

She looks around, wiping her eyes, and heads over to the bedside table. Quietly opens and closes the drawers, one by one. Then peers down the back, by the wall. Kneels and looks under the bed – just dust and a few square metres of carpet that haven't seen daylight in a long time. She gets to her feet and tiptoes round the room intently, as if her mother might have left a note or dropped something significant – knowing that her daughter might come along all these years later, looking for clues.

She crouches beside the sink and slips her hand around the back of the porcelain column, plucks up the carpet in the corner, while Denny still stands and watches. Until Yuki finally arrives at the table by the window.

She wants to consult the photograph her mother took, to be sure it's the same piece of furniture, but she left it on the bed next door, with all the others. She could easily slip back and get it, but knows that opening the door might release whatever energy is currently contained within the room and won't be found again. She tries to convince herself that she doesn't really need it. She's studied it on a sufficient number of occasions and can see that it's the same table her mother photographed, with the window open behind it and the lace curtain billowing in between.

Denny is over by the drawers now, not entirely sure what they're meant to be looking for. Yukiko lines herself up before the table, so that it more or less matches what she remembers from the photograph. Looks down at her feet. This is where she would've stood, she thinks. Then looks at the table. And that is where she sat and wrote the postcard to me and Kumi, saying that she was in Haworth and had looked round the house that belonged to the Brontë sisters. With the window open, warm air rolling in from the street and the net curtain gently buckling. And Yuki has the most powerful urge to go over to the window and close it. Despite the fact that it's already closed.

She tried to find that postcard before she came out here, and she wonders if she had found it and could now place it in the same spot where it was written whether some powerful, universal circuit would be completed, and what the psychic consequences might be.

She takes out her phone, steps back and does her best to recreate her mother's photograph. Takes three different shots and stares at each one, unconvinced. She looks around, at the rest of the room. Then turns the camera on her phone to the 'movie' setting, starts it recording and slowly pans from right to left. She watches the tiny screen as it sweeps the room. The desk, the drawers, then over to the bed, with Denny caught standing self-consciously – looking down and away. Then, with the camera still running, Yuki walks over to the bed until she catches it squarely in the camera's frame, allows several moments to pass, each marked by the flash of the small red light at the base of the screen. Then brings the filming to a close.

And yet she knows that she's failed to capture it. Not surprising, she thinks, when whatever it is she's after exists on a plane quite separate from our own. Why should I expect to draw something so unfathomable into my stupid little machine?

And then she has it.

A few months ago she discovered an online audio archive of atmospheres. Mainly modern buildings: the inhalations and exhalations of air-cons . . . the many and various hums of fluorescent lighting . . . the tonal registers of faceless conference rooms. Each location catalogued quite clinically and with an accompanying photograph. Yukiko should, she now sees, record the room's atmosphere. A three-dimensional space, into which she can later admit herself, until she's so deeply immersed that the sound will seal itself over her head.

She turns to Denny and brings a forefinger up to her lips. Then Yuki sweeps her thumb over the screen of her phone until she finds the appropriate icon and taps 'Record'. She lifts her phone above her head and holds it there, as if she's filming a concert. Or holding some industrial monitoring instrument, measuring the levels of psychic activity at hand.

How little sound two people can make, she thinks, when they put their minds to it. Although she's sure that an expert would be able to somehow identify their presence, by aural heat or shadow. But amazing also how, when the most prominent sounds are stripped away, so many tiny sounds slowly allow themselves to be heard.

A car, a couple of streets away, straining on a hill. Tight air ringing in the pipes between the radiators. The window's anxious rattle. But beneath all this, other, almost inaudible activity. The dust ever settling. The flinch of fibres in the carpet. All the hidden frequencies we have yet to identify.

Then, a minute or so into their silent meditation, another sound slowly emerges – distant movement . . . slowly assuming a rhythm. Footsteps on the stairs.

Reaching the top, then stopping. And, slower, making their way along the corridor.

Yuki and Denny turn and look at one another. Yuki still has the phone raised, just above her head. The footsteps approach, then stop, out on the landing. Denny and Yuki are both staring over at the door now. They imagine the B & B Lady on the other side. Three females of various ages, all standing and silently listening.

Yuki and Denny's attention is now focused on the door handle. What exactly do you say when you and a friend are caught illicitly sampling the atmosphere of a room that you haven't rented, as part of some private psychic investigation? What is the appropriate apology at such a time?

They keep on staring at the door handle. Almost willing it to turn. And Yuki silently drops her arm and looks at the screen on her phone, its little red light still happily flashing. I'd turn it off, she thinks, if I was sure it wouldn't make some tiny bleep in the process. Then wonders if it has a built-in limit to its recording, and what sound it's likely to make when it reaches it.

But the silence sustained by all three women continues. Could conceivably advance into eternity, one second at a time. Until at last the footsteps that had slowly made their way towards the room make their way off again, and the various creaks of the floorboards can be heard as those feet pad down the landing. Then down the carpeted stairs.

Yukiko waits as long as possible before stopping the

recording. And the phone does indeed emit a tiny squeak.

Yuki and Denny breathe again. This is too much, Yuki thinks. It must be inflicting long-term physical damage. Then she and Denny head over to the door. Yuki slips back to turn off the lamp on the bedside table. Denny eases open the door and the two of them creep back out into the world. And as they do so Yuki sees the key in the door where they left it. And thinks, What is the likelihood of someone coming along and standing right by that doorway and not noticing it?

Yukiko knew that her mother had visited the Institute of Psychic Studies when she was in London, not least because she'd talked so animatedly about the place on her return. She'd said what an odd place it was and once or twice mentioned their incredible collection of photographs without going into too much detail. So, long before she boarded the flight to Heathrow, Yuki had added the institute to her itinerary. Had found its location, looked up its opening times and worked out which day she'd most likely call.

It took Yuki two attempts before she managed to get the access she wanted. She first went up the broad stone steps on the Tuesday morning, only minutes after the institute opened. The building was part of a tall Victorian terrace just north of the Marylebone Road, with rusting railings between the pavement and basement, red-brick walls reaching up four or five storeys into the grey January sky and windows that looked as if they hadn't been washed in twenty years.

She pressed the button below the intercom, pushed at the heavy door when she heard the lock buzz open and walked out onto a cold tiled floor. The reception desk was at the far end of the lobby and Yukiko's footsteps echoed around the walls as she made her way over towards it. Halfway there she became aware of a huge portrait bearing down on her, of a man with an impressively bushy beard. He and his beard looked like they'd been around a good hundred or more years ago. The ornate frame seemed a little extravagant beside the austere expression on its bearded subject, who, Yuki assumed, must be an early pioneer of psychic thought. He sat stiffly, both hands flat along the arms of his chair, and stared off into the distance, as if daring the people who passed by to rouse him from his beardy thoughts.

From their website Yuki knew she'd have to sign in before being shown the photographs, so as soon as she and the woman behind the desk had said Good morning she was glancing around for some form or aged ledger and the pen with which to fill it out. But the receptionist insisted on knowing the nature of Yukiko's visit. Yuki apologised and fished about in her pocket for the piece of paper on which she'd written the words she knew she'd have trouble pronouncing, and slid it across the counter.

'SPIRIT PHOTOGRAPHS', it read.

The receptionist read the note, nodded and asked Yuki to confirm that she actually wanted to *see* the photographs. Well, of course I want to goddamn *see* them, Yuki thought. Why the hell else would I be here?

Yes, said Yuki. To *see* them.

So the receptionist was obliged to inform her that the photographs were in the institute's *collections* and that visitors had to make an *appointment* if they wanted to have access to the Collections Room.

It took a few moments for Yukiko to understand what the woman was saying.

But I've come from Japan, she said. Which was true. She had indeed come from Japan. Admittedly, not just to visit the Institute of Psychic Studies: she had also come to spend some time with her long-lost, condescending sister. But there was no denying her having come from Japan. If her English had been better she might have said, I am a Scholar. Or even, I am a Psychic Detective. Very well known in Japan and many other countries around the world.

But the receptionist insisted that Yukiko would need an appointment with Mr Fields, the Head of Collections, in order to see the photographs. She asked Yuki if she would like her to consult the diary and see if such an appointment might be made. Yuki said she would. The receptionist opened up a great slab of a diary, slid her finger down the page and seemed almost disappointed to find that there was a slot available the following morning. Yuki was asked if she'd like to take it. She nodded and made a mental note of it. Then turned and prepared to go clattering back across the tiles, when the receptionist stopped her.

You know, she said, you're more than welcome to visit the library. You don't need an appointment to go in there.

So Yuki followed the receptionist's directions and found her way through to the library. As she entered, a woman who was returning some books to the shelves turned and looked over, and Yuki thought she might have to endure another little interview, but the librarian just smiled and nodded, then turned back to the shelves.

The room was tall and long, reaching off in both directions, and, like the rest of the institute, felt damp and somewhat neglected. Dark wooden shelves covered all four walls clear up to the ceiling, which was about three times Yuki's height. The floor was covered with threadbare rugs and carpet and there was a faint smell of tobacco smoke.

For a while Yukiko drifted up and down, trying to make sense of the various categories which were written out on small cards and attached to the shelves at regular intervals, wondering at the sheer number of damp old books on show. They must have had to reinforce the floor, she thought. With steel. Or concrete. She advanced and allowed her finger to trail along the books' spines – *click, click, click* – thinking as she did so, Perhaps my mum called in here when she paid a visit and trailed her finger along the very same books.

After she'd wandered around at floor level for several minutes and pulled out five or six books from the shelves she thought she'd like to explore the library's upper reaches. She'd noticed a set of wooden steps with a post standing proud of the top step and small metal wheels at the bottom of one pair of its legs. She went over, climbed the first few steps and picked over a couple of shelves, just to see how much the thing was liable to wobble. Then resolved to move the whole contraption a metre or two, in order to get to some of the more interesting-looking volumes above her head.

It wasn't clear where she was meant to take hold of the ladder, or how to shift it. She sensed that the librarian, wherever she'd got to, was monitoring the situation – that this was a test of Yuki's initiative and that her performance might well have a bearing on how much deeper into the establishment she'd be permitted to go. So she gamely took hold of the steps and tried to shunt them, but only rucked the carpet in small folds beneath its legs and it took Yuki a while to work out that she should go round the other side and tip the vertical posts towards her, bringing the wheelless legs up off the floor to allow a little movement. The wheels squeaked as she shuffled backwards, pulling the steps after her. She had to keep glancing over her shoulder to check she wasn't about to hit a wall or knock some potted plant off its pedestal. As long as I don't actually pull the goddamned thing right over, she thought – as long as I don't end up pinned to the floor beneath it, I shall consider it a success. And she succeeded, in those terms at least, in dragging it into what looked like a more promising neighbourhood, set it down, then gave the whole thing a little jiggle, to check its steadiness, before finally climbing up the steps.

The books grew dustier and more obscure as she ascended. Many had been covered with transparent plastic, now grey and opaque with age. Some of the spines were held in place with ancient strips of tape.

The titles didn't make a whole lot of sense to Yuki, so she brought out her phone and consulted her English–Japanese dictionary. There were a fair number of 'Paths' and 'Pathways' in the titles. Also a good deal of 'death', along with its denial – as in 'No to Death' and 'Death is Not the End'. The covers sometimes gave an indication of the content – a misty mountain top . . . a net curtain billowing in a window . . . geometric shapes which revealed themselves to be optical illusions – but nearer the ceiling the books grew dark and solemn, as if they considered illustrated covers a little frivolous.

Clutching the upright post, Yuki reached out and plucked two or three books from the shelves, quite randomly. A fine grey dust lay across the top of their pages. Inside their front covers a small rectangle of the institute's own headed paper was glued to the right-hand page, and on it were stamped the dates on which the books had last been taken out: 10th May 1974, 2nd April 1966 and, in one instance, 25th June 1954. Yuki climbed to the very top of the wooden steps, her hand clamped around the wooden post, and felt as if she'd reached the threshold of some vague and dusty portal, tucked away beneath the ceiling's flaking paint. For a moment she saw herself as if from a distance. This is where I am with my investigation, she thought. On the cusp of revelation, or quite possibly oblivion. Teetering on a half-built bridge.

*

The day of Yuki's second visit to the institute was an even colder, greyer affair. So dismal, in fact, that by the time she'd walked all the way out there and climbed the front steps of the beleaguered building she wondered if she had the strength to force herself through its doors. The same receptionist buzzed her through. The same big-bearded gentleman sat and gazed out from his portrait. Having signed in, Yuki was instructed to sit beneath him on a wooden bench. So for a while she and the bearded fellow sat and stared into the distance together, both wondering what the future had in store. After three or four minutes Yuki heard a clatter of footsteps coming across the tiled floor towards her and looked up to see a slightly younger man than the one above her, and not quite so beardy. They shook hands, he introduced himself, then led her past the reception and into the gloom.

Halfway down that dimly lit corridor he turned and pulled back an old wooden door, but it wasn't until Yuki came alongside him and saw him drag a metal grille from left to right that she understood that this was an elevator. They stepped inside, Mr Fields slid the grille back, pressed a button and they started to ascend. It was the slowest elevator Yuki had ever encountered. She thought, We'd have been quicker taking the stairs. She pictured the wooden box in which the two of them stood dangling at the end of an ancient rope.

As they rose, creaking and bumping, through the middle of the building Yuki could see the plaster of the elevator shaft creep slowly past – could quite easily have reached through the grille and written her name there so that future passengers in this wardrobe/elevator would wonder at the Japanese writing. Might imagine it to be some secret code. After they'd passed the second doorway without docking Yuki had a furtive glance up at her host. His beard still had several years' growth ahead of it before entering the bushy realms of the fellow downstairs. Who knows, thought Yuki, perhaps within the institute's walls the length of a man's beard is restricted according to his psychic status. Or perhaps a beard responds spontaneously to a man's spiritual experience, suddenly bursting forth as each new level is attained.

At the third door the elevator slumped to a halt and hung there, rattling in the shaft. Mr Fields swished back the grille, pushed at the door and held it open, allowing Yuki to step out first. Then he led her down the corridor, took out his keys and opened a door into a long room, about the same size as the library. Its ceiling was not so high and the shelves, rather than being spread evenly throughout, were crowded together at both ends. A huge old table took up the remaining space.

The room seemed very green. The table top was covered with a layer of green leather and the lampshades which hung down over it were even greener. As she edged her way round the table Yuki counted four large cast-iron radiators, each pumping out its own dusty Victorian heat. Mr Fields took her coat and pulled a chair out for her.

Now, he said, Mrs Harris tells me you're interested

in spirit photography. And he asked if there were any particular photographers or collections that she'd care to see.

Yuki had only landed in the UK a couple of days earlier. She understood maybe half of what Mr Fields was saying, and was having to speculate about the rest.

My mother, she said, then stopped.

She gathered her thoughts and tried again, doing her best to tell Mr Fields how her mother had once visited the institute. Then raised both hands, with all ten fingers and thumbs splayed out.

Your mother visited us ten years ago? said Mr Fields. Yukiko nodded at him.

Yuki had had weeks – months, even – to practise her part in this conversation but, judging by the expression on Mr Fields's face, most of her words failed to put him in mind of the word she was after and the ones that did didn't seem to appreciate each other's company. But she persevered and, one way or another, she thought, managed to convey the most significant point: that she wanted to see the photographs her mother had seen on her visit. Would that be possible?

Mr Fields seemed suddenly uncomfortable. He was sorry, he said, but whatever records the institute might have regarding their visitors and the material they requested would be confidential.

She may not have grasped every word but Yuki could tell from his face what he was saying. He seemed to genuinely regret the situation, but Yuki now sensed his attitude towards her harden, as if she were guilty of having made an improper suggestion regarding his relationship with Mrs Harris. This troubled her. I am, after all, she wanted to say, just a psychic detective trying to follow in the footsteps of her poor dead mother. You'd think a place like this would be more sympathetic to my cause.

For a while Yukiko gazed down at the old green leather, ashamed and awkward. Until at last Mr Fields said, Why don't I just bring out a few items for you to see?

Then he crept away, into the shadows at the far end of the room. Two minutes later he returned with a small stack of books propped against his chest and what appeared to be a pillow tucked under his elbow. He placed the books to one side and put the pillow squarely down in front of Yuki.

How kind, she thought. When the books, the Victorian heat and all the greenness become too much for me Mr Fields will lay my head down, dim the lights and leave me to my dreams.

In fact, she knew very well why Mr Fields had brought the pillow. These books were old and very precious. And, to confirm this, when Yuki next looked up she found Mr Fields pulling cotton gloves onto one hand, then the other. Yukiko was presented with her own gloves, and once they were on Mr Fields leaned over and picked a small book off the top of the pile.

The pillow had a shallow valley down the middle and Mr Fields carefully tucked the book's spine into that cleft before gently opening it. Even so, Yukiko could still detect a series of tiny creaks, which she assumed was either the complaints of the dried-out glue in the binding or the sound of the pages parting after being closed for so long.

This book, said Mr Fields, was one of the earliest on the subject of spirit photography. It looked to Yuki quite unexceptional, with a plain black cover and no more than a hundred or so pages of text. But in the middle were four pages of photographs, all very poorly reproduced, in which tiny faces peered out from the darkness. The faces, it seemed, had been cut out of other photographs, placed against a dark background and photographed again. The effect was not so much *ghostly*, more like a child's attempt at collage.

The next collection was of a similar standard, but by the third or fourth book semi-transparent figures began to appear, draped in linen and drifting above the sitter. These, Yuki assumed, had been produced by double exposure, but at first sight the results were a little unnerving – similar to photographs Yuki had found online, and she thought, then and now, how convincing they must have seemed when photography was in its infancy, and still considered uncompromisingly *scientific*. How it must have seemed that the previously unreachable had been inadvertently plucked out of the air.

Mr Fields and Yukiko slowly worked their way through that first stack of books, and then another, with Mr Fields meticulously transferring the books to the pillow, bobbing in and out to reveal their contents, then building a new stack on the other side. Yuki could see how much he revered these books. How he loved bringing them out for his visitors and talking about the photographers involved. After presenting his second stack he asked Yuki if she didn't perhaps wish to make some notes – even offering to provide a pencil and paper. Yukiko accepted, if only so that Mr Fields didn't think her ungrateful or that she was failing to treat the subject with the seriousness it deserved. Whereas, in truth, she could have happily sat all morning, gazing down at whatever appeared on the soft altar of her pillow, beneath the flurry of Mr Fields's soft white gloves.

After they'd worked their way through a third selection and Mr Fields went off again, Yukiko sat back in her chair and looked around the room. Her mind already felt packed with pictures and she wanted to briefly contemplate something else. When Mr Fields reappeared he was carrying two small photographs, one in each gloved hand. He nudged the pillow to one side and placed the first photograph on the table – a rather stern-looking woman in her sixties sat with her hands folded in her lap. She wore a dark woollen twin set with a soft, flat collar. A row of covered buttons ran down the jacket's trim. Her hands were almost manly. Or, perhaps, swollen and arthritic. Everything about her was grey and unassuming, except for a necklace, a ring on one finger and a buckle at her waist. And yet she was enveloped in something flimsy. As if she had been photographed through the fine spray of a waterfall, and when Yuki followed it back to its source, she found the face of another woman, half-shrouded and facing off to the left. A dark-haired girl, barely there but for the eyes, nose and lips. And Yukiko thought, What an odd combination – this transparent, half-formed beauty and beneath her this rather cold and fierce-looking individual.

Yukiko found herself more intrigued by the real woman than her accompanying ghost. Her face looked as if it had been cut from stone. Yuki leaned in, examined her closely and discovered one other source of light, to go with the necklace, the ring and the buckle. She had a glint in her eye, defiant. As if to say, You see her, don't you? You dare tell me that you don't.

Mr Fields informed Yukiko that her name was Ada Emma Deane. He placed the second photograph on the table beside her and tapped his finger under the first one, then the other.

She took *this*, he said.

Ghost aside, the first photograph was quite a conventional portrait, but no matter how hard Yuki looked at the second one she found it practically indecipherable. All she saw was a mist or blizzard, with the stark outline of a leafless tree off in the distance. The lower half of the picture might have been a cobbled street or beach of shingle. But, as Yuki stared at it, the cobbles or shingle were gradually transformed into a vast crowd. Hundreds, possibly thousands, of heads and faces, all packed together. This was, Mr Fields explained, a very particular occasion – a service in memory of soldiers who had died in the Great War. Not a funeral, he emphasised, but a service held in their honour. Mrs Deane was in attendance and she took the photograph as the crowd stood in silence. Then Mr Fields reached in and with his gloved finger hovering over the photograph indicated a line of shadows above the heads of the crowds.

The soldiers, he said. The ghosts of the dead service-men.

Yukiko leaned right in, until she could feel her own warm breath come back up off the table, and finally was able to make out a line of dismal forms, hunched forward, as if they were marching. Well, that would make sense, she thought. That all these people gather to bow their heads and think about the poor, dead fathers, sons and uncles. And, without even knowing it, conjure up their ghosts.

She was still hunched over the tiny photos when Mr Fields slipped away again and this time was gone for quite a while. When he finally returned he was carrying a selection of dusty albums. He moved the photographs aside and retrieved the pillow. Settled the first album onto it and eased its pages apart. The photographs were as small as the last, like miniatures, but laid out six to a sheet. In each shot, it seemed, some forlorn-looking individual perched on a chair while a veiled creature floated about them. But these were more elegantly composed and altogether better executed.

Yukiko studied the expressions of the subjects, trying to gauge whether they were in on the deception. Possibly not, she thought. But when Mr Fields replaced this album with the next and drew back the cover, Yuki found a set of pictures which were quite different from the rest. Well-dressed men and women faced the camera in groups of three and four, their hands folded in their laps or holding the hand of the person next to them. The prints had the same ochre tone as a leaf which had given up its last drop of chlorophyll. The men and women all looked quite formal, but somewhere in each photograph was a small, intense ball of light. It was stronger in some than others but in every image clearly illuminated the neighbouring air. And this ball of light seemed to Yuki more arresting than any number of ghostly faces. More chillingly convincing. That what had been caught was not a face up against the veil that separates our world from another, but an unknown and uncompromising force.

Yukiko sensed that Mr Fields was watching her. When she finally turned he indicated for her to accompany him and led her over to the far end of the table, where he crouched down before a great wooden plan chest which was tucked beneath it. He ran his finger down the labels, then pulled a drawer out. He picked out one print, then another – quietly chatting to himself as he did so – then laid them out on the table top.

These prints were much larger than the others and, judging by the subjects' clothes and the quality of the photographs, more recent. Mr Fields turned to Yuki. These are *very* rare, he said.

Yuki nodded, to show that she appreciated the gravity of the situation, but it was only later that she understood he may also have been saying that they were rarely seen.

Yukiko moved quietly in alongside him. The photographs appeared to have been taken at séances or meetings of some sort and from the outset Yuki saw that they were different in another regard. All the stillness and reverie was gone. These images were packed full of action and random energy, the participants caught in a flash, with tables and chairs flying, as if in the midst of some strange electrical experiment. Most of the figures weren't seated or static. One or two may have held hands around a table but most were up, out of their chairs, leaping and stumbling – with the camera right in among them. Participants were caught, eyes closed and open-mouthed, among the chaos. Not at all sure what was happening, or what was in the room with them.

Mr Fields undid a ribbon from around a cardboard file and took out a clutch of photographs in which a middle-aged woman sat with a shawl up over her head, like a South American peasant. Her eyes were closed and she was grimacing, as if undergoing the most terrible anguish or ecstasies. In the next, a woman was drooling, eyes popping, her breasts spilling out of the top of her blouse. Everything was strained and full of discomfort and Yuki saw how there was an illicit thrill in viewing these images – something wild, even sexual about them, akin to an anthropologist's photographic record of some far-flung primal ritual. It wasn't till much later, as she lay on Kumiko's couch and struggled to sleep, that it occurred to Yuki what else these images reminded her of. She'd once seen a collection of photographs of individuals incarcerated at a lunatic asylum – desperate, vulnerable people. Intentionally or not, these psychics and mediums were mimicking the tortured souls of those disturbed and uninhibited inmates. Which helped lend credibility to the idea that these spirits were with them – *in* them – and, whether their host wanted to help them or not, were insisting on being known.

Mr Fields seemed to sense Yukiko's discomfort. There are worse, he said. But perhaps we should save those for another time.

He was about to add something when a telephone rang somewhere off in the shadows. Mr Fields went in after it. Yuki could hear him talking. And when she next saw him he seemed quite excited.

Do excuse me a minute, he said. But we've had a little delivery.

He slipped away. In truth, Yuki was grateful for the respite. On the whole she believed herself to be capable of considerable mental stamina, but each series of photos had seemed to land a blow on her. She also suspected there was something faintly toxic about them. Something darkly unpleasant that she didn't want to get too deep into her.

She walked round the table, just to stretch her legs, and

came to the stacks of books where she'd originally sat. She bent over them and sifted through them in her cotton gloves. Then thought, What's the likelihood of me ever seeing such pictures again?

She knew she should wait and ask Mr Fields's permission. She also knew there was a good chance he might refuse. So she went over to her jacket, took out her phone – and crept back. Then took as many photographs as she dared.

When Mr Fields finally returned, beaming and carrying a package, Yuki was back over by the plan chest. She sensed that Mr Fields's attitude towards her had softened. And not just because of his delivery, which he set down at the far end of the table. He raised a finger. One minute, he said. Then headed off towards the shelves again.

Yukiko looked round the room. Wondered if this was where Mr Fields spent all his time, in this green half-light. Whether it had been his predecessor who'd met her mother or Mr Fields himself, with even less of a beard on him.

Your mother, Mr Fields called out. How long ago did you say she visited us?

Yuki squinted and could just make Mr Fields out, in a small pool of lamplight, picking away at a pack of index cards in a small set of drawers.

Yukiko explained, as well as she could, that her mother had come over to the UK in the summer, which meant that it was probably a little more than ten years ago now.

Mr Fields continued picking through his index cards. Then Yuki saw him stop and, a moment or two later, heard him say, *Well, that's odd . . .*

He stumbled away, even deeper into the darkness, and finally re-emerged carrying a plain A4 folder. He made some space and placed it on the table, pulled back the cover and for the first time that day Yukiko saw a non-Western face staring back at her. What's more, it was a face with which she was vaguely familiar.

Have you heard of Tomokichi Fukurai, Mr Fields asked her. Yukiko nodded. She'd seen a similar, if not the very same photograph whilst carrying out her own research, with his hair combed back, a tiny moustache and pair of thin-rimmed spectacles. He had an air of faint amusement, but there was nothing ghostly about him, and no ghosts anywhere else in the frame.

And do you know his work, Mr Fields wanted to know.

Yuki wasn't quite sure. Over the years she'd read a good deal about spirit photography, but her research hadn't followed any particular form. She'd read accounts of the experiments Fukurai had carried out with Koichi Mita, not least the one in which they tried to conjure up an image of the far side of the moon. She had also skipped through a rather dry book of his in which he described how his experiments were carried out. But she had him firmly fixed in her home country and hadn't expected to encounter him over here.

Mr Fields mimed taking a photograph with an invisible camera, and shook his head.

Mr Fukurai didn't use a camera, he said. Then brought a flat hand up beside Yukiko's temple.

Just *photographic plates* . . . to try and capture people's thoughts.

Yuki knew something of this. It was the kind of notion that at one point in the day seems almost reasonable and at another quite ludicrous.

Now, did you know that Professor Fukurai came to England?

Yuki didn't. In fact, she was sometimes inclined to imagine that her parents were the first Japanese people ever to set foot on British soil.

Then Mr Fields strolled around the table and picked up one of the photographs of balls of light hovering between a group of people.

William Hope, he said. One of the best-known British spirit photographers – invited him over in 1928 to deliver a lecture at the International Spiritualists' Federation. Then up to his home in Crewe, to carry out some experiments.

Yukiko was still staring at the photographs, baffled. Mr Fields looked steadily at her.

I think perhaps this is something your mother might have been interested in, he said.

Yuki and Denny lock the bedroom door and tiptoe back along the landing, with Yuki convinced the B & B Lady is loitering somewhere in the shadows, thinking, What the hell is that Crazy Jap Girl up to in my house?

Back in Yuki's room Denny climbs up on the bed, stretches out and stares at the ceiling. Yuki still has the key to her mother's bedroom in her hand, growing warm there. Will have to put it back on its little hook at some point. But not now, she thinks, when the B & B Lady is hanging around, waiting – ready to leap out at her.

Of course, this could very well be the same key her mother used when she stayed here. In which case, couldn't there perhaps be some vestige of motherly kindness buried deep in it, beneath the heat of however many hundred other guests have used it since? Then Denny calls to her. Yuki turns and finds Denny sitting up on the bed now, pointing. Yukiko looks down and sees a patch of blood on her trousers about the size of the palm of her hand. At first it seems that bloodstain might be a manifestation of some psychic encounter. The kind of thing Mr Fields might have in his collection. And Yuki is still staring down at it, dumbfounded, when Denny comes over, takes her hand and leads her back to the bed.

As she limps along Yuki thinks, Well that's kind of interesting. It didn't bother me at all until I saw it. Now, suddenly, it hurts like hell.

She undoes her belt and the button at the top of her trousers and Denny carefully pulls them down, clear of the wound. The tissue she'd packed against it is soaked right through with blood and peels away with the trousers. The wound is all puffed up, kind of shiny, and the four neat holes are leaking blood.

Maybe it didn't like you moving around, says Denny.

But Yukiko isn't listening. She's thinking, So, this is it – me bleeding to death in a B & B in Brontë Country. Soon the B & B Lady will knock at the door and present me with some Victorian chaise on which various other female guests have passed away.

Denny's over at the window now, looking out at the snow, still falling. I'd take you to the A & E at Leeds, she says. But we'd be slipping and sliding all over the place.

Denny's thinking – seems to fairly brim with purpose. OK, she says, and goes back over to Yuki. Helps her pull her trousers back up. She looks around for Yuki's coat and is buckling her belt when she suddenly stops, lifts her head and looks her square in the eyes.

You're not gonna faint on me, are you? she says.

When they step out into the street it feels a whole lot colder. The snow's already thick on the ground and shows no sign of slackening. One or two cars still creep along the streets, but with great care now, and Yuki and Denny advance with similar caution, their every fifth or sixth footstep shooting away from them, which is not what Yukiko wants at all.

Yuki holds tight onto Denny's forearm as they make their way slowly down the steep high street. Across the road they see an older woman slip and fall and other people go hurrying over to her, and Yuki thinks, If we do manage to get down this hill, there's no guarantee we'll ever get back up it.

At the bottom Denny leads Yuki onto a quieter street where the falling snow has the place pretty much to itself. A hundred metres or so along it they arrive at a doctor's surgery, which is not a whole lot bigger than the little houses on either side. Denny goes up to the door and pushes at it, but it's locked.

The surgery's opening times are stencilled onto the glass in the door in silver letters. Denny peers at them, then pulls her phone out of her pocket. Says they must only have closed a couple of minutes ago. Then she puts her face up against the glass and stares down the corridor. There's someone in there, she says. I can see them wandering around. And she starts hammering away at the glass.

Eventually, a disgruntled-looking woman appears and announces, muted through the glass, that the surgery's closed and what time it's going to reopen later on. But Denny turns and points over at Yuki. She's hurt herself, she says. She's bleeding. Then turns to Yuki. Open your coat, she says. So she can see the blood.

It's pretty impressive. The woman goes off and a minute or so later, reappears, opens the door and leads them through to a tiny waiting room, where they have to sit and fill out various forms. Magazines are stacked up on tiny tables and in one corner is a pile of brightly coloured children's toys. Yuki looks at the magazines and toys and imagines all the bacteria and viruses smeared all over them, incubated in the radiator's heat.

Once the paperwork has been thoroughly checked and sanctioned, Yuki and Denny are shown through to the surgery and before they've even taken a seat Denny is talking to the doctor, as if she's Yuki's personal interpreter. Telling him about the dog and how it came galloping over towards them. How it leapt up and bit Yukiko, while the two of them were out having an afternoon stroll.

The doctor asks Yuki to undo her trousers and gets her to lie down on a sort of gurney. He pulls on a pair of latex gloves, rips open a sterilised pack and uses the folded cloth to wipe away the blood.

That's a nasty bite, he says.

Denny's right beside him, peering in at the bloody, puckered holes. I'm thinking it was maybe some sort of wild dog, she tells the doctor. A wolf, maybe.

The doctor stops for a moment and looks over at Denny. Then goes back to cleaning the wound. Well, whatever it was, he says, if I were you I'd report it to the police.

He asks Yukiko if she's planning to stay in town long,

and suddenly Denny is stock still and silent.

One day, she says. Maybe two.

The doctor says, OK. Tells her he's going to dress the wound and give her a tetanus shot, but that she might want to take a regular dose of paracetamol for a couple of days, just to keep on top of the pain.

Denny seems almost disappointed. As if she's been imagining Yukiko confined to bed, in a fever. Her bringing Yuki her meals on a tray. The doctor gives Yuki the shot in her good thigh, hands her a card with a phone number on it in case things suddenly worsen, and a couple of minutes later she and Denny are back out on the street.

The snow has stopped and the town is perfectly still. As if the snow has quietly stolen something away, but with such delicacy that people aren't inclined to mind. As they walk along the street Yukiko thinks, In the Beautiful Decrepit Future this is how it will be. Pristine and a little terrifying.

The cars have abandoned any hope of climbing the high street and the pavements have become so treacherous Yuki and Denny have to make their way from the window ledge of one shop to another.

Halfway up, Yuki stops to catch her breath and Denny asks her how her leg is feeling. Yukiko looks down at it. Thinks, It feels much the same as it did half an hour ago, but now the other leg's hurting, where the doctor stuck me with a needle. So I'm basically limping with both legs.

It's OK, she says.

Yuki spots a teashop over the road and suggests they go on in, just to warm themselves up. So they creep across the cobbles, with Denny holding onto Yuki's arm, order two coffees and take a table near the back. The place is dimly lit and the only window is the one out onto the street which instils in Yuki the feeling that she's in some sort of cave-cafe that's been carved right out of the hillside.

Yuki checks her phone. There's a text from Kumiko wanting to know when Yuki's going to get back to London. Yuki thinks, I'll deal with all that later on. And since the phone is in her hand she tries to find the recording she made in her mother's bedroom, to check that it's actually picked up something. She locates the file, presses 'Play', and she and Denny lean in and listen, picturing the two of them standing there, breathless and anxious. A girl brings their drinks over and slips the cups and saucers onto the table as they listen. Yuki's convinced she can hear the car pass by in the distance and, a few moments later, footsteps as the B & B Lady approached. She looks up and nods at Denny. Denny smiles and nods back at her. And the two of them sit there, listening to the recording of the two of them standing and listening. Watching the door. Waiting it for it to swing open. And they feel some of that same anxiety sweep back over them again.

When the recording finally ends they both sit back for a moment. Denny looks at Yuki and asks what she was hoping to find in the bedroom. Yukiko's not sure –

and even if she knew she's not sure she'd know how to articulate it, in English or Japanese. So she picks up her phone and opens up her photos and scrolls back through them – the ones she took at the parsonage . . . her hotel room in Leeds . . . Kumiko drunk . . . Kumiko pulling faces . . . Buckingham Palace . . . right back to the ones she took at the institute, of Mr Fields's precious photographs.

She's looking for a shot of an old couple sitting upright, with a small globe of light between them. But before she can find it, Denny leans forward and asks Yuki to slow down so she can have a better look. There's the shot of Ada Emma Deane, bristling beneath a shrouded beauty. The headscarved woman, wincing and writhing, as if possessed. Denny swears under her breath. And when an image sweeps onto the screen of a group of people holding hands around a table, and a buttoned-up woman at one end with her head tipped back and her mouth half-open, Denny reaches out and places a finger on the head of the medium.

So that's why you booked yourself in at the Grosvenor? she says.

Yuki looks up at her. Doesn't understand.

The psychic, says Denny and taps the screen, so that she inadvertently opens up the image and the possessed woman slides beneath her finger. That's why you're staying at the weird B & B.

When Yuki finally grasps what Denny is saying she finds that the B & B, as she pictures it in her mind now, accommodates a medium quite easily. And given that in the last few years of her life her mother was pretty much obsessed with visions and psychics, Yuki's sure this must have figured in her decision to rent a room.

She's getting a little light-headed and wonders if this feeling – when everything seems about to come together, and she might even be levitating just a centimetre or two – really is preferable to the conviction that her investigation has reached an impasse and that there is simply no more to be done.

Denny does her best to explain that it isn't the woman who currently runs the B & B who is the psychic but that woman's mother – and that she retired some years ago and passed the business on to her daughter.

Yuki asks if this psychic's still alive. Denny nods. I think so, she says. She used to live in a home . . .

And Denny points up the hill. Yuki half turns and stares at that same impenetrable wall, as if she might now see right though it and find the old woman off in the distance, staring enigmatically back at her.

173

For old people, says Denny.

Yukiko turns back – doesn't understand. So Denny hunches her shoulders and grips an imaginary walking stick. For people who are very *old*, she says.

And Yuki suddenly sees this woman, ancient and fragile, her presence in the world hanging by a thread, and thinks, If I don't talk to her soon she'll be gone and I'll have lost the last good chance of understanding what my mother was doing here.

Can we see her? she says. Her eyes widen. Tomorrow?

Denny says, Sure. Then she turns and looks towards the window, to see how much daylight there is still out there.

Or we could go now? she says. It's only a mile or two out of town.

And so they take one last gulp of their coffee, pay and make their way up the high street – still tentative, but a little less tentative than before – then call in at the B & B so that Yuki can pick up her map and her mother's photos, plus anything else she thinks might be of use. Stuffs them in her rucksack. And the two of them head back out into the cold.

The light is already starting to fail as they leave town, and it's getting colder. Yuki looks around. Thinks, This snow isn't going anywhere. It's all going to be right here tomorrow morning, but with a layer of ice on top.

Denny says that the old people's home is not too far away, but Yuki can't tell whether this means they're going to arrive lightly chilled in fifteen minutes or frozen in an hour and a half. She's a little alarmed when Denny leads them off the road and out towards the moors again, but Denny assures her that climbing this one small hill will save them having to walk all the way round the road.

And she's right, because pretty soon they're over the top and padding down a snow-packed path with the big old house not far below them tucked among a dozen leafless trees. The lights are on in maybe half the windows, but the place looks exceptionally gloomy. And England, Yuki thinks, seems to be full of such old, exhausted-looking places which must surely have a corrosive effect on the national character.

The closer they get to the house and the old woman the more apprehensive Yuki is feeling. She asks Denny what sort of thing this woman used to do. Denny's not sure. One of her grandma's friends sometimes used to visit her but never disclosed many details, as if such revelations might displease whatever spirits she was so keen to come into contact with. But she's heard from other people that Mrs Talbot might just sit and hold your hands for a while . . . study your aura . . . ask about your past and discuss what lay ahead . . . and that after three or four sessions some other force or presence might enter the room. A force or presence, at least, that would be known to her.

Yukiko imagines Mrs Talbot reaching out to cup her cheeks in her bony old English fingers – looking deep into her – and is horrified. Not so much at the idea of the old lady delving so deeply into her, but at what abysmal horrors she might find.

They leave the path and Yuki is pleased to feel the solid road beneath her feet again. They head towards the house and pause by the stone gateposts. A gravel drive leads right up to the main door. A patch of orange light spills from the foyer onto the steps, and Yuki thinks how good it would be to find herself in that heat and light. Denny sets off, Yuki follows, they climb the steps together and have barely entered the building when a large and largely cardiganed woman steps out before them.

We're not having visitors, she says. Not for another couple of hours.

She's eyeing the two of them up now, quite comprehensively. Then says, Who is it you want to see?

Instinctively, Denny lies. My grandma, she says. Elsie Taylor.

The large woman looks back at her, even more suspicious now. We don't have any Elsie Taylors, she says. Are you quite sure that's her name?

The woman looks from Denny to Yuki, as if she's thinking, There's something wrong here. Some girl turning up at the wrong time asking for non-existent residents, with this Japanese-looking young woman who refuses to look me in the eye.

Denny feigns disappointment and says, Well, I must've got the wrong place. Then she turns and leads Yuki back to the door, down the steps and out onto the snow.

They tramp down the drive and are almost at the gate before they glance back, to find the woman still standing there, guarding the warm light. They walk out of sight, and wait against the wall until she slips back inside. Then Denny says, OK, c'mon. And she leads Yuki through the gate, round to the left of the building and under the trees where the snow is thick and smooth.

They carry on, deeper into the darkness, and are right around the back by the bins and a derelict outhouse when they reach a metal fire escape, bolted to the wall. They stare up at the steps for a moment. Denny gives Yuki a wink, then sets off up them. There's snow on each step and a strip of snow along the handrail, which is shattered each time their hands take a hold of it.

They creep up three storeys, stopping at each fire door, trying and failing to force it open. Until they're right at the top of the steps on a metal landing and feeling a cold breeze coming at them, before another closed door. Denny leans out to her left to examine the nearest window. Then, before Yukiko can intervene, she's over the rail, reaching out to the window ledge and trying to get her fingers under the bottom of the window frame.

She turns back and says, I need something long and thin – like a knife. Yuki's thinking, What do I have that is like a knife? She looks around. Is about to slip off her rucksack to look inside it.

Then Denny says, Doesn't matter.

She's managed to nudge the window up a little, then a little further. Now has both hands right through the window and transfers her weight over onto her forearms so that she's scrambling against the wall, with nothing but a long drop beneath her feet.

She crawls head first into the building and has all but disappeared from view when she clips her heel on the edge of the window frame and knocks her shoe off, which goes tumbling into the bushes below. Then she's gone. A couple of moments later, she pops her head out, panting and laughing. Yuki points at the bushes and says she'll go and get it. So she pads all the way back down the fire escape, wades into the bushes and pokes about there, but can't find Denny's shoe. She's still looking for it when Denny hisses down at her from the top of the fire escape.

Leave it, she says. I'll get it later.

Inside, the care home is oppressively humid. Smells of furniture polish and warm food. The room Denny clambered into was some sort of utilities room. The next door along has a laminated card fixed to it, with 'Marjorie' written in felt tip pen, but no accompanying surname. The card on the next door says simply, 'Gwen'.

Fuck, says Denny. What's her first name? And stares at Yuki, as if she might know.

They stand there in the carpeted corridor for a while, until Denny eventually just shrugs, knocks on the nearest door and, when a voice calls out, turns the handle and ushers Yuki in before her.

It's a small room with not much more in it than a bed and an old woman sitting beside it in an armchair. She has no book or magazine in her lap – she's just sitting there. The room's even warmer than the corridor. Denny says Hi and tells the woman that they're looking for Mrs Talbot, and the resident tries the name out for size –

Talbot? she says. Talbot? – without success. Have you not got a Christian name?

Denny shakes her head. She used to run a B & B in town, she says. A sort of psychic.

Oh, well that'll be Eanie, says the old woman, and tells Denny that her room is on the floor below.

Denny thanks her and opens the door, just as a carer heads into one of the other rooms. Denny and Yuki wait, then slip quietly out. Creep down the stairs and along the corridor, checking every door on both sides before finally finding one with 'Eanie' on it. Denny knocks and, as she can hear someone coming up the stairs, opens the door and both of them go scuttling in without waiting for a reply.

The room's the same size as the last one, but the bed is against the other wall. The woman tucked up in it is a few years older than Gwen and watches a TV that's blaring away in the corner.

Well, at last, she says, and reaches for the remote control.

It's a little while before Yuki and Denny work out that Mrs Talbot thinks they're here to feed her, or tend to her in some other way. When Denny explains that they've actually come up from town to pay her a visit Mrs Talbot's confused, as she doesn't recognise either one of them.

To try and put her at ease, Denny says, My grandma's Jean Edmondson.

Mrs Talbot nods and says, I know Jean. Is she still with us?

Denny says that she is. Then introduces Yukiko. It's really her who wants to see you, she says.

Mrs Talbot turns and has a good, long look at Yuki.

We think you met her mum, says Denny. About ten years ago.

The old lady nods and keeps on looking. I've met a lot of folk, she says.

Denny suggests to Yuki that she show Mrs Talbot some of her photographs. The old lady asks them to sit down, so Yuki takes an upright chair at the bedside and Denny perches on the edge of the bed.

Rather self-consciously, Yukiko opens up her rucksack and fishes around for her precious envelope. But for some reason she can't seem to find it. And in those few moments she convinces herself she's left the envelope back at the B & B or even dropped it out on the moors. She keeps on looking, but now imagines the photographs cartwheeling across the snow, off into the darkness. She begins to panic; has trouble catching her breath. So that by the time she finally finds the envelope and brings it out she's practically in tears.

Mrs Talbot slowly reaches out and places her hand on top of Yuki's.

You're all upset, love, she says. Is that why you've come to see me? Because you're all upset?

She slips her fingers under Yuki's and lifts her hand, as if gauging its weight, and keeps on looking right at her.

Well, getting all upset will get you nowhere, she says. And she gives Yuki's hand a little squeeze in her own small hand. So why not show me your photographs?

Mrs Talbot releases her hand and Yuki draws out the photos and slowly leafs through them – settles on the one of her mother standing by the front steps of the Grosvenor and hands it over. Mrs Talbot takes it from her and brings it up to her face.

Yes, she says, and nods, still peering at the photograph. Yes, that's right.

And this is almost too much for poor Yukiko – the simple acknowledgement that her mother really has been here and spent some time in the company of this old woman. Her ghostliness falls away and she now walks along the cobbled streets with solid purpose – resurrected, for her two or three days in Haworth, about which Yuki, Kumiko and their father know so little. And Yukiko finds herself longing to be there with her, her own arm tucked through the sleeve of that lost cream coat.

Mrs Talbot sits and waits, watching Yukiko. And, little by little, Yukiko returns to the room. Denny can see that Yuki is not about to do much talking, so she leans over towards Mrs Talbot and says, She thinks her mum stayed in a room on the first floor, at the far end of the landing.

I couldn't say, says Mrs Talbot. But I do remember her. And me sitting with her, maybe two or three times.

Denny says, Do you remember what you talked about?

The old woman looks back down at the photograph. It's a while back, she says. Then turns to Yukiko. This is your mother, you say?

Yuki nods.

And now she's gone? says Mrs Talbot.

Yuki nods again.

Mrs Talbot asks to see the other photographs, so Yukiko hands them over and the old woman works slowly through them – Yuki's mother outside the parsonage . . . the desk by the open window . . . the still, black reservoir – without uttering a word. But when she sees the twisted tree out on the moors she scowls and brings it up even closer. Well, yes, she says. I *do* remember her.

She turns to Yukiko. She wanted to know about my visit from that Japanese man.

Mrs Talbot sits and stares at Yukiko, waiting for her to help her out.

The man who came up with Mr Hope, she says. Who took the photographs. When I was a girl.

Yukiko's quite lost. Yet, even as she sits on that upright chair, quite adamant in her ignorance, the image of the man with the neatly trimmed moustache and the upright collar begins to take shape in her imagination.

She almost laughs, incredulous, even as she suggests it. *Fukurai?* she says, and has to repeat the name twice before Mrs Talbot recognises it.

That's right, she says. Mr Fukurai.

Like Mr Fields at the institute, Eanie Talbot pronounces the name with an emphasis on the first vowel, but it's close enough for Yukiko to know that they're referring to the same man. She tries her best to digest this information but keeps thinking, How could this old woman possibly have anything to do with Tomokichi Fukurai?

182

From her meeting with Mr Fields, Yukiko is aware that William Hope invited Fukurai to the UK, to some convention, then up to his home in Crewe. But what Mr Fields hadn't mentioned was how the two men, along with their assistants, had driven up to Haworth to meet a young girl who'd recently been reported as having exceptional gifts.

When I was five or six, says Eanie Talbot, I saw an old man on the stairs at my neighbour's. A tall, old fellow, with a walking stick. And the woman whose house it was swore blind no man with a stick had climbed those stairs since her father had lived with her fifteen years before.

The following year she noticed how she had a tendency to get a little dizzy at particular locations and once or twice heard voices – not speaking to her directly, but just merrily chattering away. Then, one day, while she sat on a bench outside the Old Bull, waiting for her mother in the shop across the road, she heard a woman's voice, quite sharp and clear.

A young woman, she says, but age-old. And no idea, really, what she was saying. Just that she was talking to me from a long, long time ago.

She must've mentioned this to her mother. How could she not have? And her mother in turn must have mentioned it to Mrs Marshall, who happened to know a member of the Crewe Circle. Then, quite soon, Mr Hope, Mr Fukurai and their two assistants were heading up to Haworth in their motor car.

The first thing young Eanie Talbot knew of her visitors

was when her mother dressed her in her best clothes one Saturday morning. Some very important men, she was told, had come to town to see her. They were interested in the voices she'd been hearing. They were interested in her.

Hope and Fukurai must have arrived the previous evening because they were on the Talbots' doorstep soon after breakfast: Mr Hope and his assistant – a rather stern lady with a large bosom – and Mr Fukurai, who had a Japanese assistant of his own. Mrs Talbot can clearly remember everyone squeezing into the parlour, all six of them. Mr Hope said they'd heard about the wonderful things she'd seen and heard around the village and that, with her consent, they thought they might take some photographs while she was listening out for voices and such like.

She remembers William Hope being quite friendly. He may even have made a joke or two. Then Eanie and her mother were led down to the Bull, where the men had rented the upstairs room, which was already half-full with their equipment. Seeing it all laid out made Eanie nervous, not least because it seemed she might be about to undergo some sort of medical procedure. Mr Fukurai must have noticed, because he told her, through his assistant, that all the equipment was simply for taking photographs and promised that what they proposed to do wouldn't hurt or be remotely unpleasant. Then they sat her on a wooden stool.

It's a long while ago, says Mrs Talbot. But I remember

how all the curtains were closed. And them all standing in a circle around me – and holding hands, including my mother. Mr Hope saying a prayer of some sort. Then he and his lady assistant singing a hymn.

They pulled the covers from the big old camera and dimmed the gas lamps. Then everyone slowly slipped away into the shadows and Eanie was all on her own. One of the men asked her to think about the voices she'd been hearing lately and see if she could do her best to try and hear them again.

Denny looks over at Yuki and asks if she understands what Mrs Talbot is saying. I think so, she says. And for a while the three of them sit there, imagining little Eanie sitting on a stool, in a darkened room.

Well, I was so anxious, Eanie says. I remember someone saying I'd have to sit still or that I'd spoil the photograph, then Mr Hope's assistant coming over and showing me a picture in a book – of three young women all sitting together. And her asking if I knew who they were. Well, I didn't. And Mr Hope saying, All the same. Have a good look and, if you can, try and think about them while we take the photographs.

So Eanie held onto the book, the grown-ups went to their stations and silence descended. Mr Hope stood beside the camera, and placed a hand on the shoulder of his assistant – to keep himself steady maybe, or possibly to earth himself against whatever unseen forces were about to be unleashed. He closed his eyes . . . reached out his other hand and removed the cap from the camera . . .

held it aloft for ten or fifteen seconds . . . replaced it. Then opened his eyes again.

In all, Eanie thinks, they must have taken half a dozen photographs, each time slipping a heavy glass plate into the back of the camera. Then they put the covers back over all the apparatus, and Mr Fukurai told her, via his assistant, that they were now going to take another few photographs, without any camera being involved.

Young Eanie had so vague a notion of what taking a photograph might normally entail that this didn't strike her as particularly strange. Again, they said, all she had to do was sit and listen out for anything that might spring up around her – voices, etc. Then Mr Fukurai opened a small crate and pulled out a flat square package, wrapped in brown paper. He brought it over and, again through his assistant, explained that this glass plate had been specially prepared to pick up whatever was in the atmosphere, including any powerful thoughts that Eanie might have. He was simply going to hold it up by her head to see if it caught anything of interest. As before, she was assured that there was not the slightest risk of her coming to any harm.

Mr Hope's assistant again had Eanie look at the picture of the three young women. Then she was asked to close her eyes and do her utmost to listen out for whatever else might be in the room. She sat quietly and sensed that the Japanese man had come and stood quite close to her. She was aware of something being brought up next to her head. The way it obstructed any sound from that

186

direction. It may even have brushed against her hair.

Once or twice she dared to peek and saw someone tiptoe in, take away one package and hand Mr Fukurai another. And at some point, for the first time that day, she thought she had the sense of something stirring. Not the men, their assistants or her mother. Not below them in the pub or out in the street. But something which somehow managed to have one foot in this world and the other in a quite, quite different place.

She kept her eyes tight shut and kept on listening, until someone told her she could stop. Then, as she sat there blinking on her little stool, she watched Mr Hope and Mr Fukurai slip behind a curtain in the corner, into what must have been some sort of improvised darkroom.

When she next saw Mr Hope and Mr Fukurai they seemed quite pleased. She was shown the photographs they'd just developed. One in particular was, she was told, very good indeed: on an otherwise plain dark background was the vaguest outline of what looked to Eanie like a circle, but tilted a little, so that it was almost oval.

Eanie was asked what it put her in mind of, and with a little encouragement she identified it as a ring. Then she was again presented with the picture of the sisters and asked if she'd been thinking of them when the ring came to her. Eanie thought perhaps she had.

She was asked if she'd been drawn to any sister in particular? So she had a good look and picked the one whose face she liked the best, which seemed a popular choice. Then her mother helped her on with her coat and everyone headed out.

She's quite sure it was her first visit to the parsonage. She now assumes Mr Hope must have arranged a private tour, since the place was practically empty. He and Mr Fukurai led Eanie from room to room and she was asked to listen out for anything unusual. But she found the place not the least bit welcoming and was looking forward to getting back out into the daylight as soon as possible.

They seemed to call in at every sitting room, scullery and pantry before finally arriving at an especially dark little room. In the middle was a table with a tiny notebook on it. Eanie was led over to it and Mr Hope explained how it belonged to one of the girls who used to live there. She was encouraged to touch it – to place the palm of her hand right down on it – while Mr Fukurai, the two assistants, her mother and one or two people from the parsonage all looked on. Years later, she says, she finally understood their intention – that they saw her as a sort of spiritual bloodhound. They wanted to give her a good, strong sense of what they were after. Then, having drawn a bit of a blank in the parsonage, they took her out onto the moors.

Well, they walked and they kept on walking – seemed to Eanie to walk right through the afternoon. She would, she thinks, have been too big to be carried, but still small enough to be tired out by such an undertaking. Mr Hope had a map which he kept consulting. Every now and then they'd stop – by the rock . . . the little bridge . . . then up at Top Withens – and they'd ask Eanie to close her eyes. And Mr Hope's big-bosomed assistant would read aloud from a book that she'd brought along – the old words delivered with such gravity that Eanie assumed they were from the Bible or some other religious text.

Despite all this, any long-lost voices refused to manifest themselves. Eanie and her entourage seemed to have been criss-crossing the moors for hours and she'd grown weary. In fact, she's not sure she was meant to have stopped at all, when she began to feel quite peculiar. She stepped off the path and rested her hands on her knees. Thought for a moment that she might be sick. It would have been all the miles she'd walked. Or all the adult attention, which she still contends isn't necessarily good for a child that age. She remembers Mr Hope and Mr Fukurai coming closer and watching. Her vision seemed to come and go. There was a moment of great, great upset. Then it slowly subsided and people began to move back in towards her. Asking if she'd seen or heard anything. In fact, she didn't know. All she knew was that she didn't feel at all well, and didn't like it. Then Mr Hope and Mr Fukurai went off on their own to talk among themselves.

She remembers complaining to her mother about being so tired, and her mother promising to ask the gentlemen when they thought they might be able to go back home. Then Mr Hope came over and asked if Eanie could tell them anything in particular about what she'd seen or heard just now. And, perhaps because she really had been thinking about it, and perhaps because she remembered how pleased they'd been when she mentioned it earlier, she said she thought she might have been thinking about the ring.

This news generated a new round of excitement. There were more huddled whispers, much tramping about whilst staring at the ground. At some point Mr Hope announced that they should find a way of marking this spot, so that they could return to it later. Someone suggested stacking stones into a small cairn. But it was Eanie's mother who strode over to what was at the time just a sapling, with only a couple of branches sprouting from it, and began twisting them into a knot.

Eanie recalls seeing her mother take hold of the branches and fold them together. Remembers thinking that the bush couldn't possibly want to be tangled up in such a way. Then she felt strange again. Very strange. And it was like a curtain coming down. A great and heavy curtain, and she was gone.

When she finally opened her eyes she was on her back among the heather, bewildered and crying, with Mr Hope and Mr Fukurai quite excited and her mother all upset. It was a good few minutes before she felt any better and was slowly brought back up onto her feet. Then, with her mother propping her up on one side and Mr Hope's assistant on the other, they began to make their way back to town.

Of course, her fainting did nothing but bestow extra

significance on the location, but Mrs Talbot's presiding memories are of discord, confusion and wanting only to be safely back in her own home.

She doesn't remember seeing Mr Hope and Mr Fukurai again after that afternoon. They escorted her to her front door, then her mother took her upstairs and put her to bed. A week or so later she and her mother received a letter expressing their gratitude. She still has it somewhere. She has no idea if they ever returned to that spot on the moors, or what they did with the photographs. And she hadn't thought about that day in a long time until Yuki's mother came along.

Later on, of course, she'd be out on the moors and see that bush, with the two main branches entwined, and be tempted to undo them. But she never did. And soon the knot was too strong and quite beyond her, and just seeing it would bring back that unsettling feeling. So she'd do her best not to pass that way again.

For a while Mrs Talbot and Denny and Yuki all sit in that small room in silence. From the rest of the building muffled sounds slowly make their way through to them: a door slamming . . . voices . . . people coming and going. And Yuki suddenly feels tremendously tired. This place is so goddamned hot, she thinks. I feel like I'm being drugged.

Denny says, So what did you talk about with Yuki's mother?

Eanie says, Well, she was mainly interested in Mr Fukurai. Wanted to know every last little thing.

Then she looks over at Yuki and says, You know she was having visions of her own. That she was *seeing* things.

Yukiko stares back at her and finds herself nodding. Her mother would sometimes discuss such things quite openly – at dinner, or sitting in front of the TV. Yuki hated it.

Mrs Talbot leans forward and picks out one of the photographs – of Yuki's mother standing outside the B & B.

Shall we see if I can contact her?

She looks up at Yukiko. Shall we see if she's there?

She drops the photograph into her lap and takes Yuki's hands again. Studies every inch of her face.

Oh, I can see you in her, she says. I really can.

Yuki is not sure that she likes this.

Denny says, What did she see? What kind of visions?

But Mrs Talbot doesn't answer – is too busy with Yukiko. So Denny leans right over and tries again.

You said she was having visions, she says. What kind of thing did she see?

Mrs Talbot pauses, with Yuki's hands still in hers, and turns to Denny.

A girl, she says. A young girl.

And she looks back at Yuki.

Someone from the family, she says, and nods.

What had been distant sounds in other parts of the building have slowly grown closer. Knocking at doors . . . the hum of conversation . . . doors closing. Denny, at least, is aware that there are now members of staff on this floor, advancing towards them. She gets to her feet and tries to pull Yuki up with her. But Mrs Talbot still has hold of her hands.

Are you sure you don't want me to try and find her, she says.

Denny is picking up the photographs and stuffing them back into their envelope. Finally, she takes Yuki's hands and draws them out of the old lady's clasp.

The bush, she says to Mrs Talbot, and holds up the photograph. Do you remember where it is?

She has Yuki's map now. Is opening it out on the bed.

The knocking on doors is getting closer. Yukiko stands by the bed, as if in a trance.

By establishing the location of two or three landmarks, Denny manages to pinpoint more or less where the bush might be. She takes a pen from a jar on the bedside table. Pops the top off and makes a cross on the map.

Then there's a knock at the door which goes some way to bringing Yuki back to her senses. Instinctively, Mrs Talbot says, Come in. And a young woman in a pale blue uniform pops her head round the door and starts to tell Mrs Talbot what's for dinner, before noticing Yuki and Denny.

Oh, sorry, she says, as if she's interrupting. But then her attitude suddenly changes.

She pulls her head back out and calls down the corridor. Mrs Weaver – there's someone in Eanie Talbot's room.

Denny has just about tucked the last of Yukiko's belongings back in her rucksack. But Mrs Talbot has reached out and got a hold of Yuki's hand again.

And I see her in you, you know, she says.

Denny can tell how much this is freaking Yuki out – how it's not really helping.

That little girl she saw, Mrs Talbot asks her. Do you know who that might have been?

Then Denny grabs hold of Yuki's arm and drags her out through the door. The young carer is waiting in the corridor. Denny and Yuki step past her to find the large woman who blocked their way at the entrance heading towards them, with the stairwell beyond. She looks as if she wouldn't have any problem at all in grabbing a person and bundling them to the ground. Looks as if she'd positively enjoy it.

So Yuki and Denny turn and head off in the other direction.

You damn well stop! the large woman calls down the corridor.

And when Yuki glances over her shoulder, she sees her come charging after them, just like a bull.

They hit the fire door and go tumbling through it, and suddenly all the heat and light is gone and they're out into the cold, cold darkness. They fly down the steps, slipping and sliding, with Yuki struggling to keep a hold of her rucksack. Just about manage to get all the way down without falling and breaking a leg. When they reach the ground they stop and look up to see the woman leaning over the railings, calling down to them.

Denny piles into the bushes after her lost shoe. And seeing that they still haven't gone, the large woman begins to head down the fire escape. Denny looks and looks, until the woman's almost on them. Then says, Fuck it. And she and Yukiko run off across the snow, laughing and shouting. Round the side of the building and out onto the road.

*

They're still breathless and giddy five minutes later. The memory of the woman coming charging after them proves hard to shake. But pretty soon Denny limps to a halt, lifts her shoeless foot and tries to rub some heat back into it between her hands.

Oh, man, she says, staring down at it. My entire leg's gonna drop off before I get home.

Yukiko offers to try and carry her but, as Denny points out, she can barely walk herself. So they carry on along the pavement, rather than over the hillside, which is now almost completely lost to view.

They limp from the light of one lamppost to another, until finally they're back at the top of town. Denny points down the street she has to take, but before she goes checks that Yuki has her photos, map, etc. and insists that she makes a note of her mobile number. So Yuki pulls out her phone and taps Denny's number in.

Promise you won't go looking for the weird bush

without me, she says. We'll go out and find it tomorrow.

Yuki promises.

Then Denny limps off home down one street and Yukiko limps down another, back towards the B & B.

Yukiko has always known that her mother leaving the car door open was significant. She sees the car now, with the driver's door open, the keys in the ignition and the snow falling. Surely, someone contemplating taking their own life would slam it shut, or possibly even lock it. As a way of expressing just how firmly their mind had been made up. But since the door was left open Yukiko has often wondered if perhaps her mother pulled over and stepped out for a moment's reflection. Just wanted to stand there in the snow. So that her final moments would have been a sort of euphoria, rather than some dreadful diminishment – some slow and awful snuffing-out.

Having talked to Mrs Talbot she now wonders if it could have been a vision of the young girl that drew her out of the car and in among the snowflakes. She saw the girl, or thought she did, looking lost and desperate, pulled over, and when the girl went off, she simply went on after her. The curtain of snow closed behind her and she was lost herself.

By the time a passing motorist saw the car, pulled in and approached it, the snow had covered the seat and half the dashboard – had found its way into the folds and gullies around the base of the handbrake. So straight away he must've known that there was a problem. Would have known it the moment he saw the open door.

By the time Yuki reaches the Grosvenor Hotel the sky is black and solid above the streetlamps. She heads straight upstairs, turns on the TV and climbs into bed. Thinks, Apart from being half-frozen – and my ass, where I got bitten on one side and jabbed with a needle on the other – I feel pretty good. I practically have an appetite.

She checks her texts and messages. Considers waiting a while, until she's good and ready, then thinks, If I don't call her now I'll never do it. So she turns the volume down on the TV and brings Kumi's number up on her phone.

Where the fuck are you? says Kumiko, without even a Hey or How you doing. I've been leaving messages for you all goddamned afternoon.

Yuki's already decided just to go right ahead and tell her where she is and what she's doing. Because, really, what can she do but scream and shout?

I'm still in Haworth, she says. In my big old bed, watching my tiny TV.

At the other end of the line there's a colossal Kumiko Silence. A great yawning chasm of resentment, sucking the rug, the bedspread, everything into it.

You said you were coming back *today*, she says quietly. We made an *arrangement*.

Yuki thinks, Well, no. *You* made the arrangement, but then I went ahead and chose to do something else.

I got bitten, she says. This huge great dog jumped up and bit me in my ass, out on the moors. I had to go to the doctor's . . .

Kumiko interrupts, but Yuki's determined to finish.

. . . and have a shot in the other ass. So now I'm hobbling around like a goddamned penguin.

Kumiko's stopped talking. Has reinstated her Almighty Silence.

Yuki lets this stand for a while. Shakes her head and rolls her eyes to herself. Eventually says, I'm sorry, Kumi. I just didn't have enough time to do everything I wanted. I'll get the train back in the morning.

Nothing.

Anyone else, she thinks – even a complete goddamned stranger – would've asked about the dog bite and offered a little sympathy. So she just sits on the bed and lets her sister seethe – can feel the bitterness burning down the line. Another minute, she thinks, and maybe she'll start to calm down.

Anyway, she says, all upbeat now. I found out some stuff about Mum's visit. I met this old woman who saw her when she was up here. A sort of psychic. They had these long talks about the visions Mum was having . . .

Then out of nowhere Kumiko comes storming back into view.

Yukiko, she says. Do you honestly believe that there's something out there – something you're going to find or someone's going to tell you – that is going to fix things? That's going to make everything all right?

Yuki does her best to remain calm. To push on through this. You're not listening, she says. This woman actually sat and talked with Mum, three or four times – about Fukurai and all sorts of other stuff. I always thought Mum came up here because of the Brontës, but she didn't. She came to see this woman. To talk to her about her visions . . . about what was going on in her head.

That's because she was *mad*, says Kumiko. How long before you accept that?

Yukiko just about manages to stay on her feet and keep on going.

She told me, she says – louder now to try and block out whatever Kumiko's saying. She told me how Mum had said she kept seeing this young girl everywhere.

It doesn't matter, says Kumiko.

Yuki's doing her very best not to lose her temper. Well, of *course* it fucking matters, she says. Her wandering off and leaving the car door open. She was probably just chasing after the girl . . .

She was *mad*, says Kumiko.

Stop *saying* that, Yuki says. Not when we could've *done* something. Got her better help . . .

It wouldn't have made any difference, Kumiko says. She'd've still ended up killing herself.

201

That's not true.

Yes it is.

You don't know that. How can you say that?

And it's as if, having contrived to bring Yuki to this very point, Kumiko now can't help but take a moment – to consider the power she has and any last reservations – before bringing the whole world down on her.

Because she tried to kill herself the year before, she says.

Silence.

That's not true, says Yuki, trying to fend it off.

Dad told me, Kumiko says.

And then it's done.

Yuki says, That's not *true*, again, but is already falling – the door slammed shut on her.

She screams, hits the phone – twice, three times – trying to end the call. Then hurls it across the room.

It strikes the wall and comes apart. And Yukiko folds in two, as if someone's punched her. Feels herself being filled right up, with something poisonous. And there's no letting it out. It's already in her, raging away.

She tries to scream it out of her, but whatever it is restores itself with every breath. She's against the bed. Climbs up onto it, tries to lie down and bury her head in the sheets but her body won't allow it. So she gets up and blunders, wounded, round the room.

She keeps moving, moving, but in her mind she is deep down in the reservoir, with everything inchoate and pressing in on her. Her mother, sister, father, all roiling, tumbling. And not enough air – nothing like enough air at all.

She finally comes to rest standing over her phone, on the floor in pieces. Briefly wonders if the B & B Lady heard her scream and is now on her way up. She bends down – carefully, so as not to spill herself. Picks up the pieces. She tries to reassemble them, in a kind of trance: the phone's outer casing, the battery, the battery cover. And as she does so, so her conversation with Kumiko is reassembled, and the deep black pit opens up again.

She thinks, I've gotta get out of this room. Is beginning to worry about her own well-being. Wonders if she should maybe try and get back to London tonight after all. Get to London, take a train straight out to Heathrow, and just sit and wait for the next available flight.

She finds her coat and keys. Then heads out onto the streets.

This pain, she thinks as she walks along, it's just as real as when that dog sank its teeth into me. I can feel it in my chest, in my head, all the way out to my fingers. It just goes on and on.

She pictures Kumiko and her father confiding in each other – over the phone, in the kitchen. And her mother. The number of hours I've spent trying to find her, to redeem her. Half my goddamned life.

She limps along, without knowing where she is or where she's going. Until at last she arrives at a T-junction and finds she's reached the edge of town. Beyond the road there's nothing but fields, off into oblivion. She stands there, staring out at it. The cold, black night, with the snow packed hard beneath it. Then she finally turns and walks back into town.

By the time she arrives at the narrow lane that runs alongside the graveyard it feels like some of the adrenaline is receding, leaving a solid block of anger. She walks up to the gate and the big, blank wall of the parsonage. The sisters who lived here now seem utterly unknown to her, unimaginable. In fact, the whole town is suddenly odd and unfamiliar, as if the world is one great lie. She looks around and feels the cold moving in on her. Pulls out her phone. And within five minutes Denny is heading up the lane towards her, her curly blonde hair catching the streetlight – about the same place Yuki first encountered her.

She walks right up to Yukiko, a little flustered and out of breath. Asks if she's all right.

Yukiko stares steadily back at her. Shrugs. Then shakes her head.

So they walk back down the lane. Past the darkened shops. Past the pubs with their light spilling out from windows and doorways. All the way down the hill, to the shop where Yuki bought her Coke and snacks yesterday evening, and where she now buys a pack of beers. Then on, through the snow, back up to the B & B.

In her room, Yuki splits the beers and offers one to Denny, but she tells her that she doesn't really drink. So Yuki opens one up and the two of them sit, side by side, against the pillows with Yuki sipping steadily at her beer.

She's vaguely aware how Denny keeps on looking over at her but doesn't mind or feel the need to explain what's going on with her. She finishes the first beer, burps, drops the empty can on the bedside table and reaches out for another one.

At last, Denny says, Have you been thinking about what Eanie Talbot was saying, about your mum?

Yuki shakes her head. Not really, she thinks, and she pictures the old woman in her tiny room . . . she and Denny running along the corridor . . . down the fire escape.

She suddenly sits up. Your shoe, she says. And she can see it, soaked and cold among the bushes. That poor, lost shoe. She climbs off the bed and looks around the room till she finds her headtorch. Brings it up to her forehead, with the straps dangling down on either side.

We should go get it, she says.

But Denny really doesn't want to be going back out and getting all cold and wet again. She frowns, shakes her head. And for the first time she sees Yuki look at her, disappointed, which Denny finds pretty hard to take.

The room slips back into stillness, silence. Then Yuki takes the bottle of Jameson and pours a large belt of it into a glass. She heads over to the window, brings in the Coke, half-frozen, and tops the glass up with it.

She takes a couple of sips as she stands there, as if at some weird outdoor bar. Then leans right out – peers down at the pavements, then up at the roofs across the street. Denny slips off the bed, goes over and joins her.

Then the two of them lean on the sill, with the night air cold against their faces.

Yuki asks if it snows a lot up here.

More than it used to, Denny says. When I was a kid it never seemed to snow at all.

Yuki sometimes imagines a tribe of people who've never seen snow – never even heard of it. Then one day, for some reason, it starts to fall on their little village. Just imagine. They'd think it was the end of the world.

She reaches out and takes a pinch of crisp, white snow between her fingers and drops it into what's left of her drink. Lifts the glass so that the streetlight shines right through it and she can see the snow slowly melting in the whiskey and Coke. She thinks of the reservoir – imagines the snowflakes landing on it now. Onto the cold, dark water. Settling onto the surface, then gone.

She still can't understand why her mother would take a photograph of the water without it meaning something to her. The wind-bent tree . . . the open window . . . the flat, still water – they must all have some significance.

They continue to stare out of the window. Then Yuki suddenly brightens and raises a finger, as if she's just had a great idea.

She pours more Coke into her glass, drops another pinch of snow in after it and closes the window. Tops her drink up with whiskey, wanders round the room till she finds her notebook. Then takes it up onto the bed and flicks through it till she comes to a blank page. Denny climbs up beside her. Yuki has a pen in her hand and is writing out a dozen or so columns of Japanese letters. She's shaking her head, saying she can't believe she didn't think of this sooner. Then, when she's practically filled the page, she draws one last symbol at the top, which is a little larger than the others.

Kokkuri-san, Yuki says. We used to play it when we were girls.

She assures Denny that there's nothing to be scared of. She just has to remember that *Kokkuri-san* is the spirit of an old fox and must be treated respectfully. Also, not to stop in the middle of a session. Otherwise, *Kokkuri-san* won't be able to get back home and will be forced to haunt you. And nobody, except a crazy person, would want that.

Denny's not sure. Says that she doesn't really like this sort of thing. But Yuki glowers at her again and sees her flinch this time. This is what it must be like to have a kid sister, she thinks. You get to boss them around all day long.

She pulls a handful of change out of her pocket and picks out a pound coin. Then slips off the bed to fetch her precious envelope. She takes her headtorch from the top of the set of drawers, turns the main light out, flicks her torch on and climbs back up onto the bed.

She's still adjusting the torch as she settles. She smoothes the notebook flat, arranges the photographs around it and places the pound coin on the symbol at the top of the page.

All Denny has to do, she tells her, is put her fingers

on the coin. *Kokkuri-san* will take care of everything else. And when Denny again tries to explain how she finds this kind of thing disturbing Yuki looks up, says that this is *important*, and the light from the torch hits Denny right in the eyes, blinding her.

She checks over the board she's made. Oh man, she thinks, when she and her friends used to do this round at Hikari's garage they would get each other in such a state. One of the girls had so many nightmares Yuki became convinced that she'd suffered some lasting psychological damage and would wind up in an institution of some sort.

She takes Denny's hands and places the tips of her forefingers on the coin's edge. Then rests her own fingers on the other side.

She whispers to Denny, OK, so we say, *Kokkuri-san . . . Kokkuri-san . . .* then wait until he joins us. Once he's here we can ask him whatever we like.

Denny doesn't answer, so Yuki looks up, blinding her again. And Denny says, OK, *OK*.

Yuki swings the light back down onto the notebook. And, slowly, something like silence establishes itself. In time, the rest of the room beyond that small pool of light is lost to the darkness and it's as if Yuki and Denny are drifting out in space.

Yukiko says, *Kokkuri-san*, and the second time Denny joins her, in a whisper. Yuki says some more words in Japanese. Then she and Denny both focus their attention on the coin.

At last Yuki says, Are you here?

The coin remains where it is. Then Denny feels a tiny twitch beneath her fingers. And slowly, very slowly, the coin slides across the paper and settles on a symbol.

Yukiko nods. He's here, she says.

The coin returns to its original position. There's another period of silence. Then Yuki lifts her head so that the torchlight swings over to the photograph of her mother outside the B & B.

My mother, Yukiko says. Is she dead?

The light returns to the notebook – another moment or two, then the coin follows the same path as before.

Yes, Yuki says, emphatically. She *is* dead.

Denny looks up, but can't make out Yuki's face now. There's just her voice and the torchlight, pinning their fingers to the coin. Then the light sweeps off the notebook and goes from one photograph to another, as if trying to draw them all together, before settling on the photo of Yuki's mother outside the parsonage.

And how did she die? Yukiko asks.

The light swings back to the coin, which, for a moment, shows no sign of moving. Then Denny feels it pull and slowly move away. It pauses over one symbol, then slides on to another.

In the snow, says Yukiko. That's right, she died in the snow.

Denny really does wish she could make this stop now, but doesn't want to annoy Yukiko. She sees how the torchlight is on the move again – how it settles on the photograph of the reservoir's flat dead surface, catching its emulsion, so that the water almost seems to glitter in the sun.

Yuki asks aloud what her mother was doing at the water.

The torchlight swings back to the coin and, buried deep in it, there seems to Denny to be some sense of intention, but it fails to move.

Did she see something, Yukiko says. What was she looking for?

Then finally the coin sets off and slides swiftly between three letters.

The girl, says Yukiko. She saw the girl.

Denny is beginning to feel sick. She'd get up and leave, if it weren't for the dreadful fox – and the fact that her fingers are fused to the coin.

When she was here, says Yuki. Did she find what she was looking for?

Another pause. And, again, the coin appears to be deliberating.

When, finally, it moves, Yuki seems genuinely surprised.

Wrong question, she says – to Denny, to herself.

She thinks for a while. Then finally says, In the snow back home . . .

Another pause.

Did she mean to do it?

And now Yuki and Denny can both see her out in the snow, lost and frightened.

Please don't, says Denny.

But Yuki ignores her.

Did she kill herself? she says.

Then they both sit and wait, until at last the coin slowly draws their hands across the notebook. They watch it gain momentum. Land on one of the letters – the one on which Yukiko knew it would land.

That's right, she says.

She sees her mother walking – leaving the car behind her. Then stopping. Allowing the snow to slowly settle on her.

Yukiko wonders if she's finally there. She sits in silence. Until she feels Denny's fingers trembling against hers. She can hear her sobbing now. Yuki looks up, again blinding her with the torchlight, and as Denny turns away, her fingers still fixed to the coin, Yuki sees how her cheek is streaked with tears.

Yuki says another few words in Japanese. The coin slides back to its original position.

OK, she says, We can let go now.

Denny pulls her hand back and breathes hard for a couple of moments. Then jumps off the bed, grabs her coat and heads for the door.

Yukiko barely has the chance to call after her. Denny's down the stairs and over at the front door before Yuki manages to catch up with her. And crying in great gulps now, shaking.

I'm sorry, says Yuki.

Denny refuses to even look at her.

What a horrible thing to do, she says.

And Yuki thinks, She's right. I'm like some sort of witch. I can barely believe it myself sometimes.

I'm sorry, she says again.

She waits. Then asks Denny to come back upstairs, but Denny still has hold of the door.

Please, she says.

It takes a while, but when, at last, the two of them go back up to Yuki's room they climb the stairs wearily, as if they've been out half the night. Yuki opens another beer and pours herself another whiskey. Then she digs down into her rucksack for her pipe. Shows Denny how to hold it, how to nip it in the side of your mouth and stare off into the distance, as if contemplating something significant. How to take it apart.

They talk a little about Eanie Talbot and her visit from Mr Hope and Mr Fukurai, when she was such a young girl. Then they lie on their backs with the main light out and Yuki slowly moves the light from the headtorch around the ceiling, and tells Denny about Koichi Mita and how he and Tomokichi Fukurai claimed to have produced photographs of the far side of the moon, by having Koichi Mita reach out for it with his imagination and Fukurai catch it on a photographic plate.

She holds the light steady on a crack in the ceiling, then turns the torch off. So that the crack seems to burn there in the dark, before slowly fading away. Does this three or four times, at different points around the ceiling. And thinks, If an image can burn itself into your mind like that, why can't a thought be strong enough to be caught in a photograph?

Then she turns the torch on and off, on and off another few times – as if quietly mesmerising herself and Denny. Until finally she turns the torch off, the darkness moves in around them, and she fails to turn it on again.

When you're out in the cold the moment you stop moving, your body adjusts its settings from that of a machine intent on action to one in something close to repose. The heartbeat slackens, slowing the tides of blood out to your extremities so that, in severely cold conditions, your fingers and toes will start to go numb. Pretty soon your mental faculties will lose their sharpness. If you speak you'll find yourself slurring. Worse, you'll be more inclined to make bad decisions.

Early on you'll be shivering, and this is a good thing, since shivering denotes a body still capable of retrieval – of being dragged back into a fully functioning state. In fact, all the above are simply the natural consequences of a body losing heat faster than the rate it produces it. When you quit shivering you really are in trouble, because suddenly it's not just your limbs that have succumbed to the cold but your torso – that treasure chest of prized possessions – and once the cold sets to work on your heart, your lungs and liver there really is no going back.

Yukiko has read how bats and bears are able to reduce their pulse and metabolic rate to such a degree that they can drift through the winter months in a sort of torpor. They'll have taken care to tuck themselves away out of the wind beforehand, but significantly they have a mechanism which allows their temperature to fall to a survivable slumber, which we humans lack. If our temperature starts to drop without impediment it will just keep on dropping. Our pulse will subside, along with our breathing. We'll feel confused and profoundly sleepy, which segues easily into loss of consciousness. Then the body is given over to the elements, which know no better and so are merciless.

It is not uncommon that, in the latter stages of hypothermia, the victim's blood vessels dilate through sheer exhaustion, allowing warm blood to rush from the body's core. They will suddenly feel as if they're roasting and be inclined to rip away their clothes. Yukiko has been assured this didn't happen with her mother, which is some comfort to her. Knowing that the last short while of her life wasn't beset with that particular torment. It allows her to imagine her mother hunched and quiet. Allows for some sort of dignified cessation. Although in the end, it is still her mother. Her mother, all alone out in the snow.

Something strange has been working its way into Yukiko's dreams, without her quite being able to comprehend it. Something musical, mechanical.

Then Denny's voice saying, *OK*. And, *I said OK*.

The middle of the night still, but the lamp on the bedside table has been turned on – is blinding. Denny makes her way round the room, pulling on her jacket, tucking her phone in her pocket. I've got to go, she says.

And she suddenly looks so very young, so deeply aggrieved at the world. The power it wields over her.

You'll still be here tomorrow, won't you?

Yes, says Yukiko.

Denny insists that she mustn't leave town without first talking to her. Makes her promise. We need to go and get my shoe, she says.

She's over at the door now, faltering, as if she's forgotten something. Until finally she walks back over to Yukiko, leans in and kisses her on her forehead. Then the light goes out on the bedside table. The door opens, closes. And Yuki is on her own again.

For a while, Yukiko lies in the dark, her stomach burning again from the beer and whiskey. Then she kicks back the sheets and creeps across the corridor to the bathroom, where she sits, shielding her eyes from the impossible whiteness of the enamel and porcelain. She puts her head under the tap and takes three or four gulps of water. Slips back to her bedroom, up into bed, still fully clothed. Then lies there, waiting for sleep to move back in on her. But within a minute knows that it's not about to come anywhere near her any time soon.

She puts a little more thought into her preparation for this expedition. Digs out a fleece. Pulls on a second pair of trousers. Checks the route two or three times before stepping out into the cold.

Once I've seen it, she thinks. Once I've gone right up and touched it, then I'll be done.

As she leaves town and walks back out onto the moor the air is still and clear around her. The temperature's dropped way down but the snow on the ground gives out a steady glow, as if charged with daylight as it fell and now slowly releasing that light back into the atmosphere.

She finds she doesn't worry about getting lost. If she misses her target, she thinks, she'll just keep on walking. Sooner or later she'll end up back in Japan. But she does worry about wolves – tucked under the snow or creeping low across it. She wonders whether the dog that bit her in the ass was ever retrieved by its owner. What if she and Denny made the dog so angry that it reverted to savagery? What if, rather than return to a fireside rug and food in a bowl, it chose a life out here on the moors, in the ice-cold air? A dog like that, in that sort of state, would be a handful – would be able to smell Yukiko and her wound a mile away.

The streetlights are way behind her before she turns her torch on. She walks along holding it up like a tiny searchlight. Then stops and pulls it over her head. It seems to slot right back into the circular groove it left there earlier. I'm like some half-human/half-robotic being, she thinks. I should just wire the thing straight into my brain.

For the first half hour or so the landscape looks pretty familiar, despite it being buried beneath the snow. The stile over the wall where Yukiko crouched and waited for the Elders to go on without her. Then up onto the ridge, before the path drops down towards the stream. Yuki had a good look at the map back at the B & B, so she's reasonably confident where she should leave the path. After a while she stops and watches her breath before her. There's a faint breeze now, cold on her face. She turns, climbs up onto the bank of the path and out into the open snow. It's a little deeper here and the ground beneath it a little more perilous. And Yuki knows that there's practically no significant feature between here and the wind-bent tree.

After ten minutes or so she reaches the end of the ridge, pulls the map out and squints down at it – at the mark Denny made on it. Trying to gauge at what sort of angle she should leave the ridge to find it. And it's in that stillness that she first senses something else out on the moors with her. She looks up and sweeps the snow with her headtorch – and catches something – but when she swings her head back, it's gone.

She does her best to calm herself down, but that brief blur of movement now burrows away into her. She's already retracing her steps in her mind, calculating how far it is back to the path, the stile, the streetlights – and how likely it is she'd be able to cover that distance before something else intervenes.

She looks around again. Then forces herself forward. The darkness feels deeper now, disturbed. She manages another eight or so steps before there's another sound, she looks up and, way off in the darkness, sees a pair of green eyes.

This is my punishment, she thinks, for being so determined to scare poor Denny.

She watches those green eyes and knows that they're not of this world. And now Yukiko fears not just for her physical being but her mind, her soul.

Then the luminous eyes blink – once, twice. And a plaintive Baa comes rolling over the snow towards her.

Wild dogs and wolves don't make a Baa sound, she thinks. And a malevolent spirit would let out some guttural howl – or no sound at all, till it was on top of you. She takes a couple of shuffled steps in the eyes' direction. Then a couple more. The eyes slowly acquire a face, a body. She's about ten metres from the creature now, which stares squarely back at her, a pair of knotty horns sprouting up from the wool on its head.

They eye each other up for a moment, then Yukiko

goes round to one side, to give it plenty of room, and is almost right alongside it before she notices the thick lintel of snow along the sheep's back. Well, that would drive me insane, she thinks, and is tempted to try and sweep it off, to make life a little more bearable for it. But then wonders if the snow might actually provide some extra insulation. Whether, perhaps, it is a traditional thing.

In Yuki's experience sheep tend to stand in your way, rock-solid, up to the very last moment when they go skittering away. But she's right beside it now with still no sign of it moving. Maybe it imagines I've come out here to feed it, she thinks. Maybe the farmer wears a headtorch and the sheep is hoping for some late-night snack.

Then, when Yukiko is close enough to see the tiny ridges and fissures on its horns – is considering reaching out and even touching it – the sheep suddenly jolts and turns. It drives its hooves at the snow, but barely moves. And as it heaves away Yukiko sees several lengths of barbed wire tangled in the wool around its backside. And, at the other end of the wire, a large chunk of fencepost dragging along the ground.

Now that it's finally making a little progress the sheep shows no sign of stopping. It struggles on, as if trying to plough its own rough furrow in the snow. Yuki follows it for a while, horrified. Mentally riffles through the contents of her pockets, her rucksack, but comes up with nothing that will cut through wire, or even wool.

After another four or five steps, she stops. Then

watches as the sheep continues to limp away from her. Pushing on and on until it's slowly swallowed up by the night. Then there's just the sound of the fencepost dragging . . . the last flash of wool in the torchlight . . . and it's gone.

Yuki stands, staring after it. Years from now, she thinks, when I'm least expecting it, that creature will come blundering back into my consciousness and scare the crap out of me all over again.

As soon as she turns back she realises she's lost her bearings. She looks around for some clue as to what direction she came from but there's nothing but snow – scuffed here and there by a rock's edge or scrap of heather. She senses the breadth of the moorland all around her, but still without feeling particularly perturbed. Like an exaltation almost, having finally uncoupled herself from all that's gone before. She stands in the snow, waiting for some almighty terror to descend upon her. But nothing happens. The stillness deepens, is all. Then she looks down at the ground, turns in a tight circle, staring into the patch of light, until at last she finds her own footsteps forming their own path back through the snow.

She follows the footprints back to the spot where she first saw the sheep in the distance, then does her best to resume her original course. Her feet are soaking now and freezing, but she's still confident she'll find the wind-bent tree, and remains confident right up to the point when the ground starts to fall away. From her mother's photograph and Mrs Talbot's description Yuki has assumed that the bush must be in a position of prominence. How else would the wind be able to make such an impression on it? She lifts her head and looks straight ahead until the light peters out in the darkness. Then she turns back and scans the top of the hill. The horizon is a fine line with the night sky behind it, until finally she sees the wind-bent tree, ragged and listing.

She trudges up the slope, and as she walks, she notices that for the first time – in years, it seems – her mother is absent. Neither drifting over her shoulder nor up ahead somewhere, formless and pitiful. Perhaps it's the booze, she thinks. Or the fact that I'm so busy just trying to stay alive out here. Certainly she couldn't countenance a permanent separation. Life without the ghost of her mother would leave her denuded, deranged.

She needn't have worried. She's barely reached the top of the hill when she feels her dead mother's presence settling back upon her, like a heavy coat. Yuki's breathing hard as she approaches the tree. Doesn't appreciate quite how tired she is until she stands there and takes it in. It's grown a little in the last ten years, but still correlates quite easily with the photograph.

Each branch is trimmed with snow, which gives it the strange glow of a negative. Yuki tramps slowly round it until it finally presents itself in the same way as the photograph. Then she moves in, as if bringing it into focus. The tree and its photograph slowly merge and she feels that at last she stands where her mother stood.

I'm so close, she thinks. As if there's nothing more than a sheet of silk between them. And it's the strangest thing, but for the briefest moment Yuki has the idea that the bush might conceivably embody her mother. That given a set of appropriate, if exceptional circumstances, Yukiko could slowly walk right into the bush, disappear from view, and find herself tangled in her mother's arms again.

She stands there, feeling the last of her body's heat being drawn out into the night. Sees herself dissipating. She takes a step towards it. Then another. Keeps on until the branches all but brush her face. She lifts an arm and reaches in through the branches, bent and knotted, like the horns sprouting out of that sheep's dim head. Then deeper, until her arm is lost to her.

And Yukiko thinks, If some unknown force were to take hold of me now and drag me in, then I'd allow it. To be dragged in, drawn right down into the ground and be gone from here.

Yuki stands, half in and half out of the bush, until her arm grows tired. Then finally withdraws it. Turns, finds a rock jutting up out of the snow not far away and goes over to it. As soon as she sits she can feel the cold come in on her. She knows there's only so long she should stay out here, but she's still not remotely anxious. She's nearer the ground now and in her torchlight she can identify the two branches Mrs Talbot's mother must have knotted, coiled together now like two huge eels.

Without ever quite being fully conscious of it, it seems Yuki has become convinced that locating the wind-bent

223

tree will complete some spiritual circuit. That some deep emotional well will be replenished. But she's beginning to suspect that, far from taking her in or offering up some revelation, the bush is doing nothing but obscure the very thing she came out here to find. And, not for the first time, she wonders why we insist on imagining that the world contrives to help and guide us, when the evidence seems to suggest the very opposite.

She perches on her cold old stone, staring at the bush, and finds herself thinking about Koichi Mita – Koichi Mita visualising the far side of the moon. And, moment by moment, she begins to appreciate that this is what she must do with this damned bush – conduct her own experiment in psychic retrieval. But where Mita drew down the details of the moon's benighted surface, she will project herself into the very heart of this demented tree and finally grasp what secrets it keeps.

She gets back to her feet, a little unsteady now, and man, but oh, so cold. Positions her feet, as if to earth herself. Imagines herself as her mother, standing there. Reaches up and turns off the torch.

And the darkness falls, cold and absolute. Her first thought is that this is too much, and she lifts her hand, ready to drag herself back from it. But in time the snow releases its cold store of light, the stars assert themselves and Yuki focuses on the bush – keeps on staring – until it finally reveals itself as what Yuki has long suspected it of being – an obstacle. An obfuscation.

With the light gone, the cold air seems to press right

in on her, and again she imagines Koichi Mita contemplating the moon the best part of a hundred years ago. Thinks, If anything, I have the advantage of being out here among the stars. I am practically celestial. She feels the universe and what it is to be universal. Sees the blank bush silhouetted before her. Thinks, It is about to turn itself inside out, in some revolting act of rupture. I'll have to witness it, but at least then I'll know.

She stands in the dark, waiting, but the door stays shut. There's not the slightest trace of what her mother saw, or even thought she saw.

Yuki's beginning to get agitated now. She needs to move around, if only to stop herself screaming, or fusing to the ground. If I had a lighter with me I'd set fire to the damned thing, she thinks. Burn the truth right out of it. So that if the people in the nearby villages happened to look out of their windows all they'd see would be an amber stain in the sky above the horizon. Tomorrow morning, there'd be nothing but a blackened stump, with the snow melted away all around it. They'd think it must've been struck by lightning. And that would be an end to it.

She wouldn't dare do that, of course – would be far too fearful of how the universe might respond. She turns her torch back on. Looks all around her, then down at her feet. What I need is some sort of UV light, she thinks, specially calibrated to pick up traces of psychic disturbance. And she wonders if it's at all conceivable that the spot where her mother stood to take her photograph might be the exact same spot where Mrs Talbot stood and fainted as a girl. It would make sense, she thinks. Her mother would be unwittingly drawn to it.

So she moves along, scanning the ground with her torchlight. Thinking, Even a scientist, surely, would back me up on this – that an event of the magnitude of Eanie Talbot fainting . . . of my own mother standing here ten years ago . . . must leave some sort of emotional deposit. She continues to walk and scan until she arrives at what feels like a place of importance. She kneels. And without quite knowing what she does, begins to clear the snow away. The soft snow on the top, then the icy, granulated snow beneath it. Keeps on digging – digging down with her cold, bare hands. Wondering if there really might be something here, after all. If not a ring – or, at least, not one that belonged to one of the Brontës – then something physical. Some sort of proof.

She scrapes away until she's right down at the frozen earth and is splitting her nails on it. Then she leans back and kicks at the ground with the heel of one shoe – then both heels together. Keeps on kicking, until at last she slumps forward, breathless.

I'm as mad as my goddamned mother, she thinks. Madder.

She lifts her face and closes her eyes to the darkness.

OK, she thinks. That's enough.

She could so easily lie on her side and pull her knees up into her arms. She senses sleep somewhere off in the darkness, finally ready to move back in on her. Instead, she warms her hands under her arms. Then finds her phone. She's still catching her breath as she hits the number.

The moment it's answered she whispers, Hi, Dad, it's me.

Hello, my sweet, he says. Where are you?

Haworth, she says and looks around. Still in Haworth.

He says it must be late and she nods. What time is it where you are? she says.

There's a short pause and she pictures her father checking his watch. Just gone 11 a.m., he says.

Tomorrow, or yesterday? says Yuki.

Well, today's Friday, he says. What day is it in the UK?

Yukiko considers this for a moment. I'm not sure, she says.

She looks out at the stars, even sharper now.

I spoke to Kumiko, she says.

I know, her father says. She told me.

And is it true?

I'm so sorry, my sweet. I'm afraid it is.

And Yukiko really has had enough – of the endless investigation. Of simply trying to keep some hope alive.

At last she says, I get to the point where I think I've nearly cracked it. Then I take another step and I'm right back at the start.

Then there's silence, reaching out into the darkness.

Her father says, You know, Yukiko, she was very ill, towards the end. We could none of us reach her. I'm not sure you're ever going to be able to make sense of it.

Yukiko looks up and there's the bush again, staring solemnly back at her, its own small abyss.

I talked to someone yesterday, she says. A woman who met Mum when she was up here.

Yuki can tell how intently her father is listening now. Mum told her that she kept seeing a young girl, wandering round the place.

There's a long pause. Then Yukiko's father says, That's right. I never mentioned it to anyone. I'd almost forgotten. She told me she thought it was maybe her mother. Her mother when she was a girl.

And Yuki sees herself sitting there in the snow, quite bewildered.

He says, She lost her own mum when she was quite young – you know that. Her father married Hisako a few years later. But she always missed her. It's not really something she talked about. I don't know why, but when she was at her worst, she started to see her around the place.

And now Yukiko is crying.

Oh, I miss her, she says. I miss her so much.

Silence.

We all do, my sweet.

Yukiko and her father talk for a little longer. Then she tells him how she's due to fly back to Japan next weekend and how she's thinking of spending a few days at home. He says he'd like that very much.

She's about to hang up when her father says, You know, Yuki, you're much tougher than you realise. Kumiko acts tough, but it's just her way of trying to keep herself safe. Your mother and I could see who you were from the very beginning. You were right there, the moment we set eyes on you.

They say goodbye. Then Yuki is back in the silence. The snow and the darkness.

And she thinks of her mother out here, looking for the ghost of her own mother ten years ago.

Yuki sleeps. And in her sleep, it seems, has spent half the night out on the moors with young Eanie Talbot and half the night walking on her own.

From a crack in the curtains a slice of daylight cuts through the room – across the desk where her mother wrote her postcards . . . the thin, dry carpet . . . and the bed where Yuki turns.

Someone is in the room with her – nothing more than a vague shape.

The door was open, the woman says.

And as she wakes, Yuki brings with her into consciousness her last actions from the previous night. Coming in from the moors, up to her room, cold and exhausted. Staring at that wall again, beyond the sink and TV. Taking the key and creeping back along the corridor. Wanting nothing more than to see the bed again – to stand beside it. But as she stood there, the linen had seemed so crisp and clean that she simply couldn't help herself. So she just slid on in.

Oh, she says, and begins to push the sheets back. I'm sorry.

But the B & B Lady shushes her. That's all right, love,

she says.

Yuki pulls herself up, so that she rests against the pillows. The B & B Lady perches beside her and points to a cup of coffee on the bedside table. Yukiko looks around and thinks, Strange, but it really does seem to make more sense with the furniture arranged this way – as if I'm on the right side of the mirror. If I'd only insisted on this room when I first arrived things might have been different. Though Kumiko would still have found a way of saying those awful things.

And the more she comes up out of sleep, the more self-conscious Yuki feels. As if she really has managed to scale the walls of the parsonage and squeeze herself into one of those ancient, tiny beds.

I spoke to my mother last night, the B & B Lady tells her. She said you called in on her.

Then Yuki remembers Mrs Talbot in her own small bed, at the old folks' home. Remembers the wind-bent tree . . . the ring . . . her mother asking about Tomokichi Fukurai. And feels all that weight and complication begin to settle back on her. Thinks, Oh, here I go again.

She must look pretty troubled, because the B & B Lady reaches out and lays her hand on Yuki's forearm. Just holds it there, calm and kind. Until, slowly, the pain begins to recede a little. And Yukiko returns to the room.

The B & B Lady says, I had a look for the letter my mother mentioned – from Mr Hope, but I couldn't find it.

Then she turns away and reaches down to the floor.

231

But I did find something else, she says.

And when she sits back she's holding a large book with a black upholstered cover, like the one that Yuki signed in the lobby downstairs. She opens it up, to a page marked with a scrap of paper.

It took me a while, she says, but I think I managed to find her.

She checks again, then turns the book around and hands it over. In fact, Yuki spots her mother's hand-writing before it's even in her lap – the only Japanese script on the page. She brings it up to her face, so she can study every stroke.

Is that her? the B & B Lady asks her.

Yuki's nodding.

The B & B Lady says, And what does she say, over here?

She points to a cluster of Japanese letters. Yukiko leans in and sweeps her finger over them.

She says she was happy here, Yukiko says.

The B & B Lady looks from the text back up at Yuki.

She was happy here, she says.

Then the B & B Lady waits, watching Yuki study the book. Until at last Yuki looks up, and the B & B Lady tells her, You know, I lost my father – when I was a little bit older than you are.

The B & B Lady shakes her head, but keeps her eyes on Yuki. I don't think you ever really get over something like that, she says.

And even as she speaks, the B & B Lady sees Yuki

begin to turn in on herself – some darkness descending.

I don't give credence to half the stuff my mother believes in, the B & B Lady says, insistent. But I do feel some part of him stayed with me.

Do you understand, she says, and waits for Yuki to look back up at her.

That he's still here, she says. And she lifts a hand and gently smacks her open palm against her heart.

Yuki sits in the passenger seat of the B & B Lady's car as they sail along the lanes – the same lanes that she came in on two days ago. The B & B Lady offered to put her rucksack in the boot or on the back seat, but Yuki likes the weight of it in her lap. It gives her something to hold onto.

She can hear the snow, wet under the wheels. But can't envisage a thaw any time soon. Looks at the snow over the fields and bearing down on the roofs of the barns and houses and thinks, It could be here for months, even years.

The B & B Lady reckons it's thirty or forty minutes to Leeds and if Yuki manages to catch a train within the hour she could be back in London by mid-afternoon, which would give her a little time on her own before meeting up with Kumiko. She pictures herself sitting in some coffee shop, looking out at the world.

The moment her phone starts to ring she knows exactly who it is. Has to heave her rucksack over to one side to get her hand into her jacket pocket.

She glances at the number on the screen before answering.

Hi, she says. And Denny says Hi back to her.

There's a short pause before Denny asks where she is – quietly, as if she's not sure she wants to know.

Yukiko tells her that she's on her way to Leeds, to get a train back to London.

I knew it, says Denny.

Then silence. And soon Yukiko can hear her start to cry down the line.

You promised, she says. You promised me.

Yukiko waits a while, then says how she thought it might be easier this way.

Denny says, And now I'm never going to see you again.

Yukiko thinks, Maybe she's right. She's not likely to fly out to Japan any time soon. And I don't intend to come back here.

So she turns to the window and brings the phone right up to her mouth, tucked inside her shoulder.

Denny, she says. You're my friend.

She holds the phone tight and looks out at the stone walls rushing by, the bushes.

And the car carries on along its path through the snow. Finally pulling away from Haworth, the Brontës, Mrs Talbot. On, then on again.

Acknowledgements

This novel was completed with the help of a grant from The Great Britain Sasakawa Foundation. The author would also like to offer heartfelt thanks to Yuko Michishita and Seiko Kato.